MW00943259

The Other Side of the Stars

by

Katherine King

The Other Side of the Stars
Copyright © 2015 by Katherine King
All rights reserved.

No part of this publication may be reproduced, stored in a retrieval system or transmitted in any form or by any means electronic, mechanical, photocopying, recording or otherwise, without the prior written permission of the author.

All characters and events in this book are fictitious. Any resemblance to real persons, living or dead, is purely coincidental.

ISBN-10: 151438020X
ISBN-13: 978-1514380208

Cover design by Ana Grigoriu
www.books-design.com

Author photo by Erin Summerill

Interior book design by
Bob Houston eBook Formatting

Dedication

For Lily, Riley, and Addy; my everything.

And for Tim who gave me my everything.

Gita

West Virginia, 1952

Chapter One

Loneliness is a simple feeling. It's not complicated like other emotions. It's a straight-edge razor kind of a feeling that cuts to your core. I never knew loneliness could feel so threatening. Never knew silence could be so loud. Besides the clock ticking and the occasional sob that escapes my lips, I'm surrounded by it. Suffocated by it.

I make myself get off the couch, get a drink from the kitchen, look out the window. Normal things I do every day, but today take an extreme amount of effort to carry out. The boughs of the globe willow sway from wind bringing in a storm. I smell the oncoming rain through the open window, see the dark, swollen clouds that have yet to release a single drop. They will soon enough. I close my eyes and inhale, thinking of my mother's face and how she loved the sweet, clean scent of the rain.

The hills of West Virginia are a broken kind of beautiful today. They shouldn't be beautiful. They're imperfect; lacking their springtime-green vegetation and lit only with grainy light from the overcast sky. But I see it.

It's time to go. I slip on my nice pair of heels, place my hat atop my head before grabbing the umbrella by the front door. I hesitate briefly before making my way to the old Plymouth.

It's time to bury my parents.

~~~~

The rain is a steady thrum against my umbrella. My hands are getting cold, but I can't bring myself to leave. An hour doesn't feel long enough to say goodbye.

The cemetery is empty except the lone gravedigger waiting on me to finish my goodbyes. He waits from a respectful distance, but I can feel his eyes on me. Normally it would make be uncomfortable, but today I don't care. Is this even possible? Could I ever really finish saying goodbye to the only two people I've ever loved or been loved by in this world? The two people who brought me into this world. The woman whose own heart pumped life into mine—whose own lungs breathed my soul to life. The man who carried me into the house after I had fallen and skinned my knees so badly I couldn't straighten them for a couple of days. He who had held me and sang to me the songs of our homeland when I was scared to come to this strange new place where faces and voices were so different from my own.

These two people I'm supposed to put in the ground, cover them with dirt and never lay eyes on them again? The gravedigger can wait.

~~~~

Maybe I'm still in shock. I can't seem to wrap my brain around the past two days. I cry, then I'm fine, then I believe it's all a lie; that my parents aren't truly dead. Perhaps it's someone else's parents and mine will return from their little drive to the lake. "We just couldn't help but stay the extra two days," Mom will say as she breezes into the kitchen; rosy cheeks touched by the sun, all smiles.

They were to drive to the lake an hour away and return that evening. Before I even expected them back, a sheriff came knocking at the door. I can still see the concern in his blue eyes, the sheriff's, when he said, "Are you the daughter of Karl and Bertha Wagner?"

I nodded, unsure of why he would be there.

He took off his hat, placed it over his heart like he was about to say the pledge of allegiance and said, "I'm sorry, ma'am. But I have some bad news. Your parents were involved in a car accident near town. A truck struck their car and..." That's when he paused as his blue eyes looked to the floor. And that's when I knew before he said the words. "I'm sorry, but they didn't make it."

I must have made him uncomfortable because I couldn't shift my gaze from his and he looked away again. I waited for him to look me in the eyes before asking, "Are you sure?"

"I'm so sorry, miss. Is there someone I can call for you?"

I shook my head as I closed the door. "There's no one."

Loneliness. I wish my parents had left me more than the mysteries of my childhood haunting me; following me through the house like ghosts I can't run from. For I am alone with my thoughts. Thoughts, memories, theories. It's enough to drive a twenty-year-old girl mad.

I dig through my top drawer past the neatly folded pile of stockings until I find what I'm looking for. The leather cover of my journal is soft in my hands as I carry it down the hall to the kitchen table. Flipping to the nearest blank page I suddenly can't think of a thing to write. I have no one to speak to. Mother and Father were the only people in my life. I have so much to say and I thought writing those thoughts and feelings down would help, but now the blank page seems so intimidating and demanding. I drum the pen on the old wooden farm table for several minutes before I begin. And then the words flow and my memories loosen and I write to say something and to have someone listen. It feels better than saying words to an empty room. Maybe if I write, the ghosts of my memories will fill up this empty hole I call a home.

You left me. You weren't supposed to leave. Now I'm alone and don't know what to do. I know how to run the farm and where the money is and how to keep food on my table. You were good teachers of the basic things. I know how to get by, but what about all the other stuff? What about life? There is so much I want to ask you both and you robbed me of that. You taught me how to survive but not how to live.

I put the pen down, unable to write anymore and go into the living room. The house makes sounds I've never heard before. The rain comes down in sheets as I sit, looking out at the empty property surrounding me. No neighbors for miles. A large garden to the side of the house. Black walnut trees scattered throughout with no pattern; not like a proper grove. The chicken coop in the back. I don't know what I'm to do. I have no job. My parents kept me from school, other kids, everyone really. I'm a woman who is as versed in the world as a child. They told me not to trust a soul.

There are no souls to trust anyhow. I am encased in a soulless house.

Chapter Two

"We can no longer call you Lidka. You are Gita now. Yes?" My mother lifted my chin with her fingers, so I must look her in the eye. *"Gita."*

"But why? I am Lidka."

She took my shoulders in her hands, holding tight. "It's a game we must play. You must never say Lidka again. Gita. Say it. Practice."

I tried to work my tongue around the new name, but it tasted funny. Foreign. I saw my mother was serious so I tried it anyway. "Gita. Gita."

"Good girl. Good. Things will be okay. Now, come try to sleep."

We were crammed against a wall below deck on a boat. It was hot and smelled. My mother was pressed against me. I'm not sure where Father was, but Mother was enough for the moment. I snuggled closer to her and closed my eyes. She was soft and safe.

"But why Gita?"

Mother whispered, "You know, Gita means song. Some songs have a beauty all their own. They can be so powerful they make you weep. That's what you are to me, Gita. Now sleep, child."

I tried, but sleep didn't come easy. There was never a silent moment there with all those people. Babies cried. Children cried. Adults cried. That's what scared me most. There were some familiar words, and some foreign to me. Someone sang to quiet their child. An Italian voice with Italian words that I didn't understand, but they sounded beautiful and warm. It comforted me even though the song was meant for someone else. I could hear the love in each phrase, each rise and dip of the sweet sound and I imagined the woman was singing to me.

~~~~

I put the radio on because I can't stand the silence. Three weeks I've been alone. I've already cleaned, baked a loaf of bread, and gathered eggs from the chicken coop. It's time to see someone. Anyone. The voices on the radio aren't going to keep me company forever.

Louis Armstrong is interrupted by the sound of tires coming down the gravel lane. I jump at the sound and run to the window. It's the postman.

Stepping out onto the porch, I let the screen door swing shut behind me just as he gets out of his truck. "Afternoon, Ma'am. Just got one for you today."

I take the letter from him and smile. "Thank you."

He gets back in his truck and I want to ask him to stay, to say more than a few words to me. I'm so desperate for human conversation that I almost can't stand it. But I let him go. When the dust settles I go back inside and look at the piece of mail.

It's from my aunt. I sent a telegram to her right after my parents died to let her know. She's the only one we kept in contact with from our homeland of Germany and suddenly her familiar handwriting sends tears streaming down my face. I ache for her, even though I have no real memories of her. Through our correspondence over the years, she has come to mean a great deal to me. The only person outside of my home whom I had a relationship with. So I ache for her; for anyone familiar. For family.

I take care opening the letter, not wanting to tear through any of the letters she has scrawled on the envelope.

My Dear Gita,

My heart breaks for you. I can't imagine being in that country all by yourself. You must be terribly frightened. I have no way of getting to you. I am too old and not well enough to sail across an ocean, but I will not let you fend for yourself. I promised your parents if anything ever happened to them I would look after you. I know you are a woman now, but you are a woman with no real life experiences. You shouldn't be alone. I am arranging for Max to come to you. He is a friend of a friend's son. He will take care of you and the farm. I know it is not what Americans do, arranged marriage, but it is all I can do to keep my word to your parents. I

send my love. Max will be arriving the week of MAY 22.
He'll contact you when he knows when his train will get
in. You'll need to pick him up at the station. He is strong
and will be a lot of help. Be good to him, Gita.

 Your Aunt Frieda

I set the letter on the table. Walk around the room, circle back to the table, pick up the letter and reread it. Then I set it down again. It is such a shock that I'm not sure how to respond. I've never even made a friend in the last several years, how does she expect me to be a wife?

 I grab a piece of stationary and start writing Frieda back to explain I don't want some stranger to come, take over and run my life. I mean, I'm lonely, but I can take care of myself. I bristle all over again at the thought of her doing this without asking me. That she thinks so little of my capabilities as a woman. What makes it her place? I talk myself down as I realize that arranged marriage is not so outlandish of a thought for her, in our homeland. But the thought of having a man here makes my stomach clench. I have no experience with men. No experience as a wife. He'll expect certain things.

 I check the date on the calendar. Double check the date in the letter. The 22nd is in two days. Two days. Perspiration breaks out on my body. I go to the window yanking it open. It's too hot in here. I can't be ready in two days. No. This will not do. No, no, no, no.

There's no time to write her. He's probably nearly here in America if he isn't already. I splash water on my face. Why is it so hot? The need to do something overcomes me so I hike up the skirt of my dress and take off running. Right out the door and through the orchard.

I run until I get to the edge of our property and can't run anymore. There's one house in the distance and I've always wondered about the people who live there. I have no idea who anyone is. No one in this entire country is my friend and the sudden realization cripples me.

I collapse in the shade of a black walnut tree and take a deep breath to calm my heart. I rest my head on the scratchy bark and close my eyes. Perhaps this will be a good thing. Perhaps he will be a wonderful man. I try telling myself this. He will be a kind man. A good one. One that will fall in love with me as soon as he sees me. The thought is almost laughable.

Then it hits me, what if he doesn't want to do this either? But, of course he does. He wouldn't come all the way to West Virginia if he didn't want to. Which makes me wonder what kind of man he is all over again. Perhaps I'm his ticket to America. Maybe he'll waltz in here, not caring if he loves me, just wanting my land and everything that comes along with a new wife...

What's done is done. I guess there's only one way to know what kind of man he is and I'll find out soon enough.

Chapter Three

The boy was a sweet one. He let me hold his tattered blanket. Told me it would make me feel better. We were in the back of a truck. I'm not sure where my parents were. But the boy, I remember him like I would remember a sweet treat. He looked just as scared as I felt, yet he comforted me. Holding onto one corner of his blanket and I another, we sat close to one another, shoulders pressed together. His big brown eyes... It makes me want to weep just thinking of them now. Where was I going in the back of a truck? I must have been small. Three or four years old. No, perhaps older. The memory's edges are fuzzy and I can only see the boy, the blanket and the truck full of people with no faces. Just the boy's. And my fear. Fear so strong it's like a noose around my neck. Those are the only things the memory holds.

~~~~

I go into my parent's bedroom where I've slept since the accident. This is the closest I can get to them now. The smell of Father's aftershave still lingers here, my mother's face cream on the nightstand. They are small, but necessary comforts. I already worry about the day I can no longer smell them. All my other senses have been stripped and denied access to them. I'll no longer see their smiles, hear their voices, touch their hands and feel their embrace, or taste my mother's cooking. But their scent clings to the room. It's all I have left.

Max.

He will be here any day now. The twenty-second came and went without word. The house has been cleaned. The garden planted. Every morning I wake, put my seamed nylons on under my dress, put on some rouge and a healthy smear of lipstick and I wait. It's now a week past when he should have been here and I'm beginning to wonder if he has changed his mind. Perhaps he got his ticket to America and once he got here, he decided there were too many possibilities. Possibilities that don't include me.

I switch the light off and lay awake for most the night.

In the morning I see my dress hanging in the closet, remove it from the hanger, but at the last minute decide against it. I'm not dressing up for someone who may never really come. The day's heat has already crept into the house, so I pin my dark curls up, tie a scarf around my head and put my working pants on. After rolling up the bottoms I head out to the flower garden. The dead rose bushes that my father refused to get rid of must go. He had hoped they would bloom again, but to no avail. I clip and pull and bleed from the thorns until they are gone and it's incredibly satisfying getting back to my routine. No more waiting on Max for me.

I just might head to town later and meet some people. I'm feeling brave and confident that I can make myself fit in in this country that I've never really gotten to know. The radio programs are the most interaction I've had with Americans since I came here seven years ago. But Mother and Father are no longer here to tell me to keep to myself. To not trust anyone. The homeland way of thinking, I suppose. There were many times during the war where Father told me people would see us as the enemy with our German accents. He didn't trust that people would figure out we're Americans now. He was paranoid for no good reason.

While I still have my nerve I run up the stairs to the house and make my way to the bathroom. Just as I'm turning on the water to the bath, I hear a knock at the door. I freeze, unsure of what do to. It can't be him; he was supposed to telephone or send a telegraph to let me know when his train would be here.

I glance in the mirror and wipe at the dirt on my face. Another knock at the door and I feel completely at a loss. I can't just leave whoever it is out there while I clean up.

I take a deep breath before rounding the corner into view of the open door. On the other side of the screen door is a man with his back to me. He's looking out toward the land probably wondering if anyone is home. I realize I'm standing here just staring when he turns around and we lock eyes.

He gives a slight smile and in a Polish accent he says, "Gita?" I wasn't expecting Polish. German, yes, not Polish. His olive skin, dark, smoky eyes make him look more French than Polish. He hasn't shaved in a while it looks like, as he has not quite a full beard. His suspenders are off, hanging at his sides and he looks as though he could use a bath more than me. He rakes his fingers through is brown hair and shifts on the porch, making the boards under him creak.

My heart skips a beat before I find my voice and I nod. "You must be Max?"

A brief moment passes before he says, "Your aunt wrote to you, I assume?"

"Yes. But I expected you a couple of weeks ago."

"I'm sorry. The ship had problems that slowed us down a bit."

"I expected you to call me. I was going to pick you up at the train station." My awkwardness comes out in full force.

"I was going to call on you, but it was such a lovely day to walk." He shrugs and shifts again. "May I come in?"

I realize I'm still standing across the room, staring like a crazy person. I cross the room and open the door for him. "I'm very sorry. You must be tired. Come in, please."

He grabs his suitcase and steps inside, looking slightly less uncomfortable than I feel. "It's nice to meet you," he says, sticking his hand out.

I take his hand and say, "Yes. You as well." I'm not sure what to do. Do I start by asking him questions? Do I offer him something to eat? Show him where his bedroom will be? Because I will most definitely not be offering him my bed.

"You'll have to excuse me. I've been traveling for so long and could stand to get a little cleaned up. Do you mind?"

"No. Not at all. Here. Come and I'll show you where you can put your things."

I feel his eyes on the back of me as I go up the stairs and I'm suddenly very aware of how I must look. I wonder if I'm what he expected as I show him to my old bedroom. "You can put your things in here."

He nods and sets his suitcase on the floor.

"The bathroom is right across the hall. Take your time."

"Thank you. I'll feel much better after I'm cleaned up. Then we can get to know each other."

"Fine. I'll put some water on. Tea or coffee?"

"Coffee. Thank you." He smiles and I find my heart jumps at the sight of it.

While I wait for him to come down, I take a dish towel and wipe at my face and the dirt on my arms. He's probably wondering what he has gotten himself into, showing up to this house with a dirty woman who just stares at him. My thoughts are interrupted when I hear him coming down the stairs, bringing the scent of soap with him. His clean shaven face accentuates a strong jawline. All his features are strong, including his lips which are almost too full, and yet it works as they balance his other features out.

"Is that for me?" He motions toward the coffee on the counter.

"Oh, yes. Here, sit. Would you like cream or sugar?"

"No. This is fine." I think I see a smile, but he looks down. There's a shyness to him that I didn't expect. It makes me instantly more comfortable since we now have something in common. "Gita. That's a pretty name."

I join him at the table and say, "Thank you."

He nods as he takes a sip of coffee.

"You're Polish." It comes out more of a statement.

He pauses and stiffens briefly before a slight smile emerges. "Does that bother you?"

"I'm just surprised. When my aunt wrote, I assumed you would be German. She said a boy she knew, so I just assumed…"

"Yes. My parents moved to Germany not too long ago. Does it bother you? That I'm not German?" His eyes settle on mine.

"No. Does is bother you?"

He chuckles and it unsettles me. I've missed the sound of laughter. Not sure how to reconcile the feelings bubbling up inside of me, I stand. "I'm sure you're hungry."

He shakes his head. "I stopped at the diner in town before coming. I can wait until you eat."

I'm not sure what to do. He's just looking at me. An uncomfortable moment passes before I say, "Let me show you around."

We walk to the chicken coop and around to the garden. "Most of the things we eat are from our garden. Come fall we bottle everything." When I realize I used 'we' and 'our' my throat tightens. I'm not ready to be emotional about my parents in front of him; a stranger. "I'll show you the barn."

We walk in silence. I'm not sure what he's thinking or feeling. I'm not even sure what I'm thinking or feeling at this point. "Father was getting ready to buy some cows. Do you know much about farms, Max?"

"A little. I worked on one for a while during the war. I'm sure I can manage."

I nod. "Feel free to look around the property. I'll go get dinner started."

It feels rude leaving him, but I have run out of things to say and I'm feeling overwhelmed. Once I get inside it's a relief to be alone again. Maybe being lonely isn't as bad as I thought.

~~~~

I was so alone, the feeling nearly suffocated me. There were people everywhere, but with the absence of my parents I was incredibly lonely. I couldn't see the boy anymore. He was taken somewhere else, but he left his blanket with me. My stomach was hollow. My tongue was thick and dry, my lips cracked. I couldn't lift myself up to see where I was. All I was surrounded by was the sound of misery. The feeling was thick and palpable and it scared me. I was too tired to open my eyes even while I cried for someone named Josef. Was that the boy's name? Someone else? I can't remember. But it's the name I kept repeating to myself. Josef.

Chapter Four

"Smells good."

The sound of Max's voice makes me jump. Looking over my shoulder as I stir the tomato soup at the stove, I see him standing near the table, looking out of place.

"Can I help with anything?"

I shake my head. "It's almost ready. Just take a seat."

After adding some basil to the soup, I give it a stir before ladling it into the bowls. I don't look directly at him as I set the soup and bread in front of him. We eat in silence for a few minutes before he clears his throat.

"This is very good. Thank you."

I nod. "The key is the cream you add to the tomatoes. And the fresh basil."

"Ah." Our spoons clink against the bowls and it is the only sound for a few more awkward moments before he clears his throat again. "I suppose we should talk about our arrangement."

My stomach drops. I don't know what to say or what is expected here, but I guess we can't avoid it forever. Another silent moment lingers on while we sip our soup. "I suppose we should go down to the courthouse tomorrow. It's about fifteen minutes away. I have no intentions of living with a man I'm not married to, so unless you have other arrangements, we will be married at once. Although I insist we get to know each other before we act married." I stand and take my bowl to the sink, not wanting him to see my face burn of embarrassment from my forward implication.

"I suppose you'll need to bring your papers along." I turn back to him to see his reaction.

He nods, making eye contact only briefly. "Okay." He shifts in his chair, takes another spoonful of soup.

"You don't have to do this." It's something I must say; my way of giving him a way out.

He finally looks up. "I gave my word. If I didn't want to, I wouldn't have come." He flashes a shaky smile, but it's a relief to hear the words, so I push the fears down. Fears that he's lying.

"I will stay as long as you want me to and help out with the farm. If you no longer want me here, I will leave. I promised your aunt that I would come and take care of you and I meant it. But the last thing I want is to be here if you don't want me to be. Is that fair?"

"Yes." It's all I can manage to say.

"Good. I think I'll finish up my soup and call it a night. I did a terrible amount of walking the last couple of days."

"You should have phoned me. I would have picked you up at the station."

He waves his hand in the air. "Don't worry about it. I wanted to have some time to stretch my legs after such a long journey."

"I need to get some rest as well. I will see you in the morning, then."

"Anything you want me to get started on in the morning? Before we go to the courthouse?" he asks.

I think about the dead cherry tree and how I had dreaded chopping it down, knowing it would take me forever to do. "Yes. The dead cherry tree on the south side of the field. Could you chop it down?"

"First thing."

I nod and leave, thinking about how Max might not be so bad to have around.

Chapter Five

Sleep doesn't come. I lie awake, staring at the ceiling. I suppose Max can't sleep either, because on the other side of the wall I hear his bed squeak as he tosses and turns. The feeling that I'm not doing the right thing comes and goes in waves and leaves me riddled with anxiety. The morning comes too soon even after the longest night of my life.

We drive to the courthouse in near complete silence with bouts of small talk about the weather, the land, things like that. The kind of things people talk about to fill uncomfortable silence, but makes it all the more uncomfortable somehow. How do I marry someone I don't even know?

The hall in the courthouse is quiet except for the squeak of shoes of the occasional person passing by. The large clock that sits over the entrance ticks as we wait to be called in by the judge. My hands sweat as I hold onto our marriage certificate, making it crinkle. Our names are there together; on the same piece of paper as if they are meant to be. Yet, it looks so foreign. It doesn't seem real or right or something. I jump when the door next to me swings open and a woman calls out our names.

Max and I don't make eye contact as we stand and make our way into the room. My heart pounds and I'm sweating under my hat. The judge speaks quickly, with no emotion and it seems fitting. I can't even listen to him, because my nerves have made it impossible. He announces us married and unlike most couples, who kiss, Max looks uncertain for a moment, then leans in and kisses me quickly on the cheek. I wonder what the judge thinks, but don't care enough to look at him again. After he signs the marriage certificate, we leave and I barely hear him mutter something about how strange immigrants are.

In the car Bing Crosby's voice croons over the radio, Dream a Little Dream of Me. "You are very quiet," Max says.

"Sorry. I guess this is just a little strange. I'm not sure how I'm supposed to act or what I'm supposed to say."

"Well, why don't we start with how people typically start off? We can get to know each other."

I nod, but the rest of the ride remains silent.

~~~~

"I hope you don't mind staying in your room for now. You know, until we get to know each other." I meet his eyes, pushing the embarrassment down. I can't be a wife to him yet.

"That will be fine."

I turn to leave when he speaks up. "How are we going to remedy that? Us getting to know each other, I mean."

I finger the button on my blouse. "I suppose we can talk."

His smile lifts the tension from the room. "Let's sit and talk then." He pats the cushion on the couch next to him and I oblige.

A very long moment passes before he speaks. "Have you been here since the war?"

I nod. "For seven years now." His eyes study me, making me want to squirm.

"You like America?"

"Yes. I don't remember much else. You know, before we came here. Even though there's a hole somehow." I glance at him and he nods for me to continue, to explain. "It's like there's something missing here. As though there's an invisible string stretched tight between me and my homeland that tugs at my heart every now and then. It's a yearning I have to a place that I don't fully remember."

"Home sickness." His voice is quiet and I see it's a feeling he's familiar with. I reach out and touch his arm, which makes him look at me. There is so much depth to his dark eyes and an understanding passes between us.

After a beat, he smiles. "We are lucky ones, Gita. We get to live the American dream, as they say. But there is love enough for our first home as well. Perhaps one day we'll go together to visit. "

"I'd like that very much."

~~~~

I don't know where these memories come from. I'm not sure if I'm making them up, or if they really did happen. They are confusing with the emotions so real and so intense.

There was a time I asked my parents about them, but they assured me they were just a dream—a terrible dream. Nothing to worry about, Father said. But the longing in my heart for the one called Josef never settled. Never stopped. Quieted some, yes, but never stopped.

I pull the tiny piece of fabric from under my pillow—the blanket from the boy on the truck—and rub it against my cheek. It's a comfort in a world of uncomfortable situations for me.

Chapter Six

I watch Max through the kitchen window as I wash my breakfast plate. He's out at the edge of the field chopping down the remains of the cherry tree. I haven't spoken to him yet this morning. I slept restlessly last night until right before dawn broke and then I overslept. He must think I'm lazy. By the amount of tree he's already cut down he must have been out there since sunrise.

I pull a piece of toast from the new popup toaster and set it on the plate with eggs and a slice of ham. The toaster was a gift to my mother from Father this past Christmas, replacing her manual way of toasting the bread on the stove. The smell takes me back to that morning when she toasted an entire loaf of bread.

I stand in the doorway, hesitating before heading out to the field.

He stops when he sees me coming.

"I have some breakfast for you when you are ready."

"That's very kind. Thank you. I could use a break anyhow." He dabs at the beads of sweat on his forehead with a rag.

On our way back to the house, he stops at the water pump and splashes water on his face and neck. "This is a beautiful piece of land you have," he says, following me through the back door.

"Thank you. Mother and Father loved it here and worked very hard to get it up and going."

"I'm sorry, by the way. About your parents. It must get lonely here with no other family. You don't have any other family here, do you?"

I shake my head.

"What about friends? Neighbors?"

"We kept to ourselves for the most part." I hand him a fork.

"How did you get rid of your accent? It's pretty much gone. As far as I can tell anyway."

"The radio programs. I would sit in front of the radio mimicking everything the American voices said. It would drive my father crazy because he wanted to hear his shows." I smile at the memory.

"It worked wonderfully. Maybe I should try that."

I shake my head. "I like your accent. Very much."

A beat passes before he says, "What was it like growing up here?"

I settle back against my chair before answering. "We were very fortunate. We had this farm and never really felt the full effects of the war. It's like my parents closed us off from the rest of the world and we kept ourselves fed and sold milk, walnuts, and eggs to get by. I think they were worried how people would treat us. It was hard to hide the fact that we were German and people automatically assumed we were Nazis as well. Or so Father thought."

He nods. Takes a long drink of milk. "Are you planning on getting more cows? I know you said your father was planning on it, but what are your plans?"

His question catches me off guard. "I don't know. I haven't really thought about it. I'm still trying to figure things out, I suppose."

"I understand. I know how hard it is to lose someone." There's a softness in his eyes for a moment before he clears his throat. "I better get back to that tree if I want it done today."

"Would you like me to bring lunch out to you? Or would you like to come in again?"

"I wouldn't mind sitting outside for lunch. But would you join me? I've spent too long cooped up on a boat with too many people I didn't want to speak to."

"That should be fine. I'll bring it out when it's ready."

He nods before ducking back outside.

"Oh, Gita?" He pokes his head back in the door, making me jump. "When does the postman come?"

"Usually afternoons. But he only comes when there's mail."

"Good. I'm expecting some letters from home and don't want to miss them."

"I'll write to my aunt and let her know everything is well. If he doesn't come, we'll have to drop it at the post office."

He smiles before disappearing again.

~~~~

Thin arms held me. "Swallow," she said. "Really easy, now. Swallow." I felt the water on my lips, but my mouth and tongue were so dry and cracked that I don't think the liquid makes it to my throat. She gives me another spoonful.

"I can't believe she's still alive. She looks dead." Father's voice.

"Shh. Don't say such a thing. She's living. Let's focus on that. You better hope for all of us that we don't get caught. If we do, we'll all be dead."

I was too sick to be scared of what they were saying or be worried about who they were talking about. Another spoonful. I felt this one slide down my throat making me cough, so Mother sat me upright, patting my back. "Easy. That's enough for now." I tried to tell her I wanted more, but I couldn't.

I couldn't figure out how I got so tired, so weak. I didn't even feel strong enough to cough so finally I collapsed against my mother's shoulder. She rubbed my back in slow, smooth circles and I don't remember anything past that.

~~~~

I check myself in the bathroom mirror before joining Max outside for lunch. I find myself wanting to look nice and wanting to him to notice. It's an uncomfortable feeling for me, even irritating at times, yet I don't resist it.

Conversation comes a little easier to us today, but it's hard to concentrate when I'm thinking about what I look like and noticing his smile and the slight dimple in his chin and the way his forearms flex when he reaches out to help me up from the grass. And the heat of his hand…

That afternoon we decide to take a trip into town to drop the letter off at the post office and to show Max around.

"Would you care to drive?" I ask Max. It seems the proper thing to do, although I haven't quite figured out if I want to do the proper thing. I feel independent, yet not so well versed in the world of courting. Although, this isn't exactly courting. I'm not quite sure what this is. I do know I want him to know that I can fend for myself. But I also don't want to be alone my whole life. There's a balance here somewhere. I just need to find it.

"You better drive. I don't know how."

I stop and turn to him. "What?"

He looks down at his shoes. "I don't know how to drive. I mean, I think I could figure it out, but I've never really driven before. Except a truck once when I was young. Anyway, I could try, I guess."

"That won't be necessary. I drive just fine. I can teach you if you'd like."

"Right now?"

"Right now."

He glances at the car, hesitating, before sinking into the driver's seat.

The way he sits, so upright and rigid makes me nervous. His hands grip the wheel until his knuckles turn white. He checks things out before finally turning the car on. We've gone over instructions several times now and he should be ready, though the way his brows are creased, I'm not so sure.

"Just remember what I told you. And relax. You're making me nervous." It's an attempt to loosen him up, but it fails.

He lets off the brake and the car rolls forward. A smile spreads across his face as he looks over at me. I return it with an encouraging nod. "Good. Now push on the gas."

He does, but it's too hard and we fall back against the seat. "Not so much."

He keeps going, turning off the gravel driveway and onto the dirt road that leads to the main one a mile ahead.

He goes too fast around the bend and the car protests. "Slow down!" I grab onto the door and my foot slams against the floor on the imaginary brake pedal.

"I can't!" His wide eyes look over at me.

"Look at the road! You're pushing the wrong pedal! The one in the middle!"

The car skids to a halt as he jams the brake to the floor and I'm pitched forward in my seat. The only sound as the dust settles around us is our heavy breathing. I glance over at him and laugh. "I thought you at least knew where the brake was."

"So did I. These American cars are different. I'm not used to it." His cheeks are flushed and I worry I've embarrassed him until he looks over at me and smiles. "That was fun. Should we do it again?"

"Ha! Not a chance. Get out. I'm driving now."

Once we've switched seats I say, "You have some practice to do before you can get your driver's license."

"Well, the student is only as good as his teacher. So what does that say about you?"

It's been a long time since I've laughed. It's freeing in a way. It breaks something loose inside of me. "Thank you for the scary ride. Now let's try to get to town in one piece." As soon as I say the words, I regret them. My parents' faces flash before me. I lose my smile and try to swallow the lump that forms in my throat.

"It wasn't that bad, was it?" He laughs again then stops when he looks at me. "Are you okay?"

I nod, not trusting myself to speak.

We drop the letter off, and I show him where the grocery store is, the bakery, and the hardware store. We speak but I've invited a huge cloud over our evening and

I'm not quite sure how to let that go. I can tell he feels my mood has dimmed and I feel guilty for it.

The ride home is quiet.

We've made it to the porch and I'm ready to go straight up to my room when he catches my arm, his fingers warm on my elbow, and I'm afraid of turning to face him.

"Gita, wait. Please tell me what is bothering you."

The tenderness in his words touches me and it's all I need to cry. "I'm just missing my parents. It just hits me out of the blue sometimes. I'm sorry."

"Would you like to tell me about them?"

His simple question releases something inside of me and I break. I'm a puddle of tears and emotion. He rubs my shoulder; I guess not quite knowing what to do. But that simple, slightly awkward touch melts my heart.

"I would love to tell you about them sometime, but I just can't right now. Thank you." Even though I want more of his touch, I let his hand slide off my shoulder as I pull away and go inside. It's not the right time for me to be thinking about Max's touch.

Chapter Seven

His rough hand softly patted my cheek. I still had no strength, but I had been keeping a little chicken broth down. Even that took me a while to be able to do. I knew it was my father's hand because of the way it scratched my skin. But I didn't mind. Just the fact that he was near to comfort me made me feel safe, better. "She'll adapt," he whispered to someone. The room was too dark so even when I mustered the strength to open my eyes, I couldn't see who was in there. "She's tougher than most the grown men I know. She'll be just fine." His words breathed new life into me. Took root, in a way. It's something I hear echoed throughout my life every time I go through something difficult. What a beautiful gift my father has given me.

~~~~

For the past two weeks Max and I have fallen into a routine. He takes care of most the farm and the walnut trees while I tend to the garden and the chickens. There are days where we finish all we can for the day and find ourselves sitting on the porch talking, usually over a game of Gin Rummy. He doesn't feel the need to fill the silence. We're comfortable being around each other without all the conversation. But I want to know more about him. It's what connects people. When you share part of yourself and then they share part of themselves. It's what I've been missing my whole life. I've spent enough time with mysterious and vague answers to questions. I need to be close to someone. And I want it to be him.

The warm evening breeze carries the sweet smell of summer nights as the crickets sing to us. I close my eyes and listen, letting my foot drag against the worn wood as we sit on the porch swing.

"What are you thinking about?" Max says.

"Just about how much I love summer and the sounds of the nights."

His eyes narrow as he tilts his head.

"What is it?" I'm suddenly self-conscious.

"Nothing."

"What do you like to do, Max? You come here to my home and you do things that belong here. What did you do before you had a farm to take care of? Tell me about your friends."

"Hmmm, what did I do?"

"It shouldn't be a hard question." His hesitation works its way under my skin. So elusive all the time.

He takes a few moments without saying anything before speaking. "I love to write and draw, though I'm not good at either. It's something I took to while going through a lonely period of time. When I needed to see a face, I'd draw one. When I needed to speak to someone or have someone speak to me, I'd write. I play the violin. Well, I did. I haven't played for a very long time. Not since I was a boy. And even then I wasn't very good." He turns to me with a smile. "Maybe I should think of something I *am* good at before I tell you everything I can't do. I can build furniture good enough."

"What about your friends? Surely you left some behind. That must have been difficult."

He shakes his head. "I haven't had any friends since I was a boy."

"You have me now." I say.

Something flashes in his eyes and I see it then; a lone soul. He still thinks of himself alone even with me sitting next to him. It hurts in a way that perhaps it shouldn't. The mood shifts, no longer relaxed and light.

He shakes his head and runs a hand down his face.

I glance away, uncomfortable. "Are you upset?"

He sighs and says, "Not upset. Just thinking."

And just like that, in a matter of seconds he has built a wall.

Just as I decide to stand, he says, "I just always figured I'd marry someone who loved me and wanted to marry me. Not like this. Not someone who was fine with me because we got along and were friends."

The words catch me off-guard and sting like a slap across the face. Where did that come from? Suddenly I feel ashamed as if I've done something wrong.

"Why did you agree to it? If you wanted love, why would you agree to an arranged marriage then? You didn't have to. I gave you a way out before we even got married. You could have left and been done with it."

He takes a moment before facing me. "It's something my mother always wanted. After the war broke out, she wanted me to come to America. To find a better life. To find a wife and get married. When this opportunity came up, I wasn't sure if I should, but…"

My neck burns in embarrassment. "But what?"

"But I needed to see if it was right. My mother didn't make it." He looks at the floor. "How could I say no to something I knew she wanted for me?"

He doesn't really want to be here.

"I won't make you do anything you don't want to do. I can take care of myself and I will be happy to let you off the hook with my aunt. You can leave tomorrow." I stand and march into the house, letting the screen door slam, only slightly muffling his calls to me.

I am such a fool.

Chapter Eight

I felt foolish. My clothes were too big for me and I was practically drowning in them. "Why are these so big?" I asked my mother.

"Well, we lost all your clothes, so we had to get more. These are all we could find for now. Don't worry. Soon, you will eat more and these clothes will fit just fine." She turned me around, gathering the back of my dress and clipped it together with a pin so it wouldn't slip off my shoulders.

I'd been ill. I was finally able to walk around, but I tired easily. I wanted to go run and play, but Mother and Father insisted on me resting for most the day. "Where are we?" I said.

"On an adventure. Do you like it here?"

I looked out the window and all I saw were fields of purple. "I guess. What are those flowers called?"

"That is lavender. Smell that." She motioned to the open window. "Isn't that a lovely smell?"

I nodded. I was only about ten years old, but I knew something was wrong. "Where's Father?"

"Away. He'll be here before you know it. Now, no more questions. Off you go. You may sit here and read or play with your dolls."

Mother never answered my questions. It seemed like forever since I'd seen my father and I worried about him. But I did as Mother said and picked a book to read. I lay in the patch of sunshine spilling in through the open window and let myself get lost in another world.

~~~~

Max is still here when I get up. I see him mowing the grass when I peek out my window. He's still here? Does that mean he truly wants to be here, or does that mean he doesn't want to back out on his word to his mother or my aunt?

I get ready for the day, make breakfast and go back into my room to read. I need to be alone for now.

A few moments later I hear Max come in, get something to eat in the kitchen and then go back outside. My eyelids are getting heavy since I didn't sleep very well last night, so I give in and close my eyes. I'm just about asleep when there's a knock at my door.

I sit up, "Yes?"

"I just wondered if you were okay. I haven't seen you yet today," he says through the door.

"I needed some time alone. I'm fine."

There's a pause. "Okay. I just wanted to make sure you knew that I do want to be here. If that's still okay with you?"

He waits for my answer. "It's still okay." I don't know why I say it. Part of me wants this over. No point in investing more time if it will end with me alone again. If I get too attached, it will be harder when he leaves. Then there's the part of me that desperately wants him to stay.

I don't hear him leave, but he hasn't said anything, so I assume he's gone. I spend the rest of the afternoon in bed, trying to sort out my feelings. By dinner time, I still haven't figured one thing out.

~~~~

"You have to make up your mind." Father held out both his hands. He promised a treat was tucked inside of one of his fists, and he was making me guess which one. I pointed to the one on the right and he opened his hand, revealing an empty palm.

"No!" I cried, even though I knew this game well enough to know whatever was in the other hand, he would still give to me.

"Give me a kiss and I'll let you have another try." He stuck his cheek out as I planted a kiss on it.

"That one," I said, pointing to the other hand this time.

Inside was a hard lemon candy. I squealed as I took it from him. "Run off and play now, I need to speak to Mother."

I do as he said and took my spot in the shade. Mother came out of the house and wrapped her arms around Father's neck. They held their embrace for a long time. I'm guessing since he'd been gone so long, they needed to. He was wearing his uniform. A red and black symbol on his arm. It was the same symbol I'd seen from time to time on flags and I wasn't quite sure what it meant.

They went inside and I could hear them talking, although I couldn't make out the words. I moved closer to the window and heard Mother crying. I'm not sure what the reasons behind her tears were, but I saw Father embracing her.

"I was so scared," she said. My mother scared? If she truly was, I'd never witnessed it. She seemed braver than anyone I knew.

"It's okay. It will all be over soon. God willing, anyway."

I decided then that there are things I would rather not hear especially if it were scary things.

~~~~

I leave the solace of my bedroom and find Max in the living room reading. He rests the book in his lap when he sees me. "I would like to apologize about last night. I don't think I said what I wanted, or it didn't come out how I wanted it anyway. I'm not very skilled at expressing my emotions."

"I'm sorry for not letting you finish. This whole thing is very foreign to me and I'm not quite sure how to do this."

He nods, accepting my apology. "Would you like to go out tonight?"

"Go out and do what?" I ask.

"We could go to a movie. I haven't been for so long. Would you like to?"

I'm a little stunned. But it thrills me. "I would love to. Let me freshen up a bit."

"I think there is a seven o'clock show. Will that give you enough time?" His smile lights up his eyes, which makes my heart thump in my chest.

"I'll be ready." Once I'm safely in the bathroom, I slow my breathing. Why is my body reacting this way? I felt we were in a comfortable place, a friendly place. Then last night I was ready for him to leave. And now the thought of going out with him sends a wave of excitement through me. I stare at my flush cheeks and whisper, "Get yourself together, Gita girl."

Chapter Nine

"You look lovely." Max's compliment makes me more nervous than I was before.

"Thank you. I'm ready if you are."

He nods, opening the door for me. We are on our way to the movie house. I think I've only been to a couple of movies in all my years. It seems like such a treat and it makes me more excited than I probably should be.

"I think I'll let you drive, if that's okay," he says, bumping his shoulder against mine.

"That is more than okay. In fact, I insist."

His laugh makes me smile. I love the fact that I can bring out such a beautiful thing in him.

In the theater we sit closer than we ever have. In the car, there's no real chance of us touching. But here…His arm is on the armrest between us, only inches away from my own and suddenly I'm compelled for our arms to touch. For my skin to feel his. I shift, moving just an inch closer, and hope it's not too obvious what I'm doing. I sit that way, not paying attention to the movie, and hold my breath. Then he moves, his elbow touching my arm and I'm paralyzed.

Another minute ticks by before he moves again. Only this time it's his hand. He rests his on top of mine and it sends a wave of heat to my cheeks. I see him look at me from the corner of my eye, so I glance his way. He smiles at me and I smile back, then look away, because it's nearly too much. The joy of this simple touch is about to put me over the edge.

It's this moment I'm firm in my decision of wanting him to stay.

~~~~

"Please stay." I clung onto my Father's uniform jacket.

"We talked about this. You know I can't."

"But I miss you when you're gone. Last time you were gone too long." Tears stung my eyes and I let them fall.

He crouched down so we were eye to eye. "My sweet, Gita. My beautiful ballad. I have to. But I promise that we will be together again soon. You must be a good girl and help your mother. Okay?"

I nodded, still crying.

"Come closer and I will tell you a secret."

I leaned towards him, loving the smell of his aftershave. "You are in charge while I'm gone. But you mustn't let your mother know. You make sure Mother is eating and happy. If you can do this, I will bring you back a surprise. Deal?" He stuck his hand out and I shook it, tears gone now.

My mother came in and handed Father his suitcase. "What are you two talking about?" she asked.

"Nothing," my father said, shooting me a wink.

I watched them say their goodbyes. Father took Mother in his arms and kissed her right in front of me. It's not something I was used to seeing, but it made me happy, made me feel safe. No more words were said, and then he was gone.

"Come, Gita. We have bread to make." Her voice was steady, but I saw a tear in her eye before she turned and left the room.

~~~~

We leave the theater holding hands, but it's too hard to hold hands while I drive, and I'm saddened by the absence I feel when he let's go. I want to feel closer to him. I want to know him. "Tell me something I don't know about you. Something you like doing."

He thinks for a minute before saying, "Like I mentioned before, I love to sketch."

"You do? What sorts of things do you draw?"

"People. They're the hardest to get right, but I like a good challenge." He smiles a wicked grin that suggests there is an underlying meaning to his words. Is he suggesting I'm a challenge?

When we get home I'm not sure what to do. We're standing in the living room, and I'm wondering if I should head to my bedroom or see if he wants to talk.

Before I get the chance to say anything, he takes my hand and says, "Would you like to dance?"

He puts the needle down on the record and the room fills with Frankie Laine singing *That Lucky Old Sun*. He spins me around, then brings me close to him. He smiles before spinning me out again. I laugh as I stumble, but when he pulls me close again, my smile falters. His eyes are intense now and I wonder if he's going to kiss me. We sway back and forth as I lay my head against his shoulder, too chicken to find out if he was going to. But this feels amazing. The feel of his body against mine warms me through to the tips of my toes. His hand against my back presses me closer. The other holds my hand pressed against his chest. He leans his head against mine. I so badly want to tilt my head back and kiss him, but I'm not that bold. Not yet.

Him holding me makes me feel loved, that he wants to be here. Maybe this is what falling in love feels like. We dance through three more songs before he speaks.

"I hope you're okay with me staying, Gita. I really do want to be here."

I look up at him and say, "Why?"

"That's not an easy question to answer."

"Try."

"Because of you." We stop swaying without him letting go of his hold on me. "I like being with you. You're beautiful. You're vulnerable, but in a strong way."

"What does that mean?"

He sighs and says, "I think it takes courage to let your guard down and let someone know you are vulnerable. You do that. I know you've been through a lot in your life, but you aren't hardened. You're so innocent. But you are very capable."

I had no idea he thought all this of me. I swallow the lump that's formed in my throat and look away.

Lifting my chin with two fingers he looks at me with an intensity again. "I hope you believe me."

"It's been such a short time that we've known each other. How did you figure all this out so soon, when I feel as though I barely know you? I want to know you, but you are too mysterious." I let this sink in before asking, "You don't speak of your family. Why?"

He stiffens. "It's too hard. I'm not like you. I have a hard time trusting people and letting them get close."

"Believe me, this is anything but easy for me. But if I don't know the real you, how do you expect me to fall in love with you?"

Something changes in his eyes. His guard goes up. "That's a good question. And one I don't have an answer to right now." He lets go of me.

"That's what you want, after all isn't it? To be in love with the person you're married to? You can try. Try to let me get to know the real Max."

But he only nods and I know I've lost him. My instinct is to feel bad for pressing the issue, but I stop myself. It's not my fault he's closed off. If he expects me to love him I have to know who he is first.

Chapter Ten

The still of the night shattered from commotion outside my door. Voices hushed but frantic, split the silence open like a rock through a plate glass window. I tried going back to sleep since I was halfway there anyhow, but couldn't. Two strong arms lifted me from my bed as I heard my father's reassuring words against my cheek. "Hush, hush. It will be over soon. Go back to your dreams, mein kleines madchen."

The next thing I remember is waking on a boat sailing from my home toward a new country.

~~~~

I wake early, and go to the kitchen to make breakfast. I'm not mad at Max, but I need him to understand something. I have feelings for him, but I can't imagine it developing into anything that will last if he never allows me to know him. I need to see below the surface of a beautiful face and easy smile. My soul needs something deeper; a connection on a deeper level.

The eggs have already been gathered for the morning and are in a basket on the counter. He must have woken up earlier than I and I wonder if he had a hard time sleeping as well. The eggs sizzle in the hot frying pan when Max comes in, holding several papers in his hand.

"Good morning."

I nod and turn back to the eggs. "Breakfast will be ready in a few minutes."

"Gita, I have something I want to share with you."

He holds the papers towards me and says, "My sketches."

I take the frying pan off the burner, wipe my hands on a towel and reach for them.

"I thought since these are something I usually keep to myself, if I shared them with you, you might understand me more. Get to know me. It's such a personal part of who I am…"

I sit at the table and look at the sketches. Each one of someone different. A man on a boat with a big nose and crooked smile—not someone you would look at and say was handsome, but Max's sketch has made beautiful. Someone at a diner or café. One is the profile of a mother reaching out and touching the cheek of her baby in a buggy. The detail he manages to put in black and white on a paper is incredible. There's emotion in the art and I feel it when I look at them.

"Max, these are beautiful. Where did you learn to do this?"

He shrugs. "I didn't really learn, I've just been drawing since I can remember. I try to see the beauty in people and put that on paper. I'm not sure if I'm successful or not."

"You are. Very much so. Thank you for sharing them with me. I would love to see more sometime."

"Those are all I have with me. I left the others behind. These are what I did on my journey over here."

"How was the boat ride?"

"Rough. Long."

I nod, remembering bits and pieces of my own journey to America. "I remember thinking we would never get here. Thinking maybe America really didn't exist and we would sail around the oceans forever. But I was young and never really heard of America before."

"I've wanted to come to America for as long as I can remember. I told my mother my plans when I was five years old and she laughed at first. But when she saw how serious I was, she told me what a great idea it was. She was a good mother. Always wanted me to follow my dreams. I wish she could see me now. She's been gone too long now. I miss her." Before emotion shows through, he shifts and clears his throat.

I had gotten the impression that she had passed away not too long ago. I must have misheard him before. He's very sincere though so I don't question him. "Thank you again for sharing with me. Let me get you a plate. Would you like a piece of toast with your eggs and coffee?"

"Please."

We make plans to get the telescope out and watch the stars tonight, and I make a plan to forget my questioning him and chalk it up to mishearing him about his mother. I need to write a letter to my aunt anyway, since I haven't heard from her in a while. Not at all since Max arrived actually. Maybe I'll ask her more about Max's mother.

~~~~

It was a blur of time after we got to New York City, then took a bus to where we ended up living; a farm with no neighbors in sight in Spencer, West Virginia. Mother and Father seemed a little more at ease then. During our travels they kept reassuring me everything was going to be fine, but they were the ones jittery and nervous. It's like they had released a breath they'd been holding for the past few years.

Mother wrote a letter to Aunt Frieda, letting her know we arrived safely.

It took a while to get settled into our new home. I went with Mother and Father into town to buy some necessary things and they instructed me not to say anything to anyone. If someone spoke to me, I was not to respond. I didn't know the language the people in the store were speaking anyway. It was different. At home Mother and Father practiced the new language with me. They taught me and had me practice every day. Every single day.

They didn't want me to have a German accent, afraid of what American's would think since the war was still going strong. I worked really hard, studying the sound of words coming across the radio. Trying to mimic the way they formed their words.

One day I heard mother in the kitchen as I sat cross-legged in front of the radio in the living room. "I had to tell her where we are. She's family."

My father grunted. "It's not safe. For her or for us. You should have told me what you were doing."

"You wouldn't have let me." My mother spoke in her serious tone, which is usually the time my father backed off.

"You're right. And there is a reason for that. For hell's sake, Fran, they could be looking for us right now. If they find her, she now has information that will lead straight to us. It's not something to take so lightly."

My mother slammed something down on the counter, probably her wooden spoon. "Take lightly? You think I've taken any of this lightly? We are running from Satan himself. We ran halfway across the globe and somehow managed to live through it. I most certainly do not take it lightly. But I felt homesick. Sick for my family who I will never see again. I made a mistake, but I will not let you make me feel bad for it. I will not let you make me feel any more scared than I already am."

She stormed past me and marched up to her bedroom, slamming the door. I heard my father sigh and go out the backdoor in the kitchen. It was rare to hear them fight. And now that I was older I began to wonder what they were referring to. There were so many secrets and unspoken things that lived under this roof and I was determined to find out what they were.

Chapter Eleven

Dear Aunt Frieda,

I am well and hope this letter finds you well also. I haven't heard from you in a long while, so I'm not sure if my letters got lost, or yours did. Max is a gentleman. We were married right away and he is most helpful around the farm. But I feel I need more information. How well do you know Max's family? When did his mother pass away? I know it is strange for me to be asking you these things, but perhaps you could give me some more insight into his home life. When I ask him, he is very brief and I feel as though he is leaving things out. I'm not saying he is dishonest, but more secretive. I'm not sure, really. He has done nothing to suggest he is anything but an honorable gentleman; it is just a feeling I get.

I hope you are in good health.
Sincerely,
Gita

~~~~

After dinner Max and I take a blanket and telescope out to the backyard. It's a perfect summer night to stargaze. The sky is clear and there is just a sliver of a moon. The warm breeze dances across my skin and lifts the edge of my skirt. Max spreads the blanket out and sets the telescope up as I sit down.

He hunches over, looking through the eye piece for several moments before he says, "Aha! Come, Gita. Look at this."

I join him and bend over looking into the telescope. "What exactly am I looking at?"

"That cluster of stars is called Omega Centauri. Isn't it magnificent?"

"Beautiful." I take a moment to marvel at the spray of light in the sky. "Would you like me to show you one of my favorites?" I ask.

"Of course."

I move the telescope around until it's pointing at Orion. I admire it before I motion for him to take a turn.

After he puts his eye to the telescope he smiles and says, "Orion's Belt," then motions for me to take another look.

As I'm bent over, I feel him reach around me so his arms are draped over me and his hands are guiding mine. "How about this one?" I feel his heart pounding against my back and I find it hard to breathe. His breath tickles my neck and I wish he'd put his lips where his breath falls.

My voice catches as I say, "Another of my favorites."

His fingers lace with mine as he straightens up pulling me against his chest, our arms crossed in front of my stomach. He begins to sway and says, "Is there any chance we can finish our dance from last night?"

Spinning around into his arms, he begins to hum as we move. The way he holds me is so tender I shiver.

"Are you cold?" he asks.

I shake my head. "This just feels really nice."

"Amazing."

We go on like this for a while. I notice where every fingertip presses. Where every breath of his meets my skin.

He spins me slowly before dipping me backwards. Before pulling me back up with our faces an inch apart he whispers, "Would you like to lay and look at the stars before we call it a night?"

Lying next to him, breathing next to him, just this touch, his hand and mine, makes me want to cry. It's something I've been craving for so long. This human connection. It's more than I could have dreamed of. I savor every minute, second, brush of skin, smile, afraid it will end too soon.

"You know what I love about the stars?"

I turn my head so I can watch him speak.

His eyes stay trained on the sky. "Not everyone will see all the beautiful marvels of the world. Never see the pyramids or set foot on Mount Everest or kiss on a bridge over the Seine in Paris. But everyone gets to see the stars. Millions and millions of stars that are thousands of light years away. Some thousands of times brighter than the sun. They're so out of reach, so magnificent, yet so accessible. A phenomenon that everyone can have a part of."

I watch the slope of his top lip as he speaks and my stomach flutters. He rambles on, and I cling to every word, loving the way he's opening up to me. The inner workings of his mind baring themselves to me. I close my eyes and pick out the rough scratch in his voice while he whispers and I drown in it.

~~~~

He walks me to my bedroom door and brushes my hair from my face. "Thank you. I had a lovely time." We laugh because it's such a ridiculous circumstance we are in. This weird dating, living together, arranged marriage situation.

"As did I."

He leans in and presses his lips to my cheek. The smooth skin of his plump lips makes goosebumps ripple down my body. "Goodnight," he whispers. And he leaves me wanting more, yet fully satisfied with what he gave.

~~~~

I found the steel box in the top of the closet behind my mother's hats. It had a lock on it that needed a key. I felt around the shelf, but there was nothing there. I went to my father's desk and searched every drawer. I hurried because they would be done working in the garden soon. They hadn't really given me any choice. I had nothing to do except wonder what our big family secret was. I couldn't find a key and time was running out, so I put the box away for the time being. I promised myself I'd keep looking for it later.

I went back to the kitchen where I was supposed to be doing the dishes and saw my father's newspaper on the table. The headline read: "Top Nazis Go On Trial for Crimes of War" with a picture of a man in a uniform that is just like the one my father used to wear. I didn't understand. Suddenly dizzy, I lowered myself into the chair. My parents had done such a good job of cutting me off from the world that I never knew the men who wore the swastika on their arms were the Nazis my parents talked about. The ones in the war that we were fighting. The ones doing those horrible things to people. It couldn't be possible. My father would spit when he spoke of the Nazis, but I'd seen him with my own eyes in the uniform.

The feeling of betrayal was real and strong. So many things had been kept from me and everything I felt like I knew was wrong. My own parents lied to me. I wasn't sure what to do with the information, so I waited on it. I would ask my father and mother when the time was right. But I wondered if they would even tell me the truth. In the meantime, I kept looking for the key to the box.

Chapter Twelve

"The storm is coming."

We both glance at the dark clouds in the sky and I nod in agreement.

"We need to get the laundry off the line before the rain starts. Could you help me?" I say, grabbing the laundry basket on the way out the door.

The wind is already blowing pretty good and snatches a shirt from the line. Max runs after it as I work as fast as I can to get the first of the four bedsheets down. I glance back to where Max went and can't see him. I feel the first few drops and shout, "Let's hurry," checking over my shoulder, but he's still nowhere I can see. I get the second sheet down and move to the third one. The wind whips hair in my face and the there's no hope of getting the laundry down before it gets wet. The clouds have opened, dumping water on me and the clothes.

"Max!" I yell and jump when he sneaks up behind me grabbing me by the waist. I slap at his chest and laugh. "Stop it. You are no help. Now all the laundry is wet."

"Then we'll hang it up tomorrow. Let's run."

"What? Where?"

He grins and grabs my hand, pulling me towards the orchard.

We run until we get to a tree for cover and I lean against the trunk gasping for air. "That was fun."

He smiles as he leans on his knees to catch his breath. His dark hair is dripping water into his smoldering eyes. His chiseled face is perfection in this moment. His smile lessens as he straightens and moves closer. The boom of thunder goes unnoticed as he makes his way to me, eyes on mine. He takes my face with one hand, threading his fingers through my hair, his thumb running across my cheekbone. "Do you still want me here?"

My breath catches in my throat. "Yes."

A flash of lightening lights up the darkened sky, but it has nothing on the electricity between the two of us.

His other hand finds my waist. "Do you want this?" I know he's talking about how close we are, about his hands on my body.

I nod.

His grip tightens and he puts his Polish lips on mine. There's a brief moment of panic on my part, not knowing what I'm doing, never having kissed anyone before, until I realize there's no reason to panic. My lips know how to respond to Max. My body understands what it wants to do. He's passion and tenderness all encompassed. I feel the need, the hunger, the wanting in his every movement, yet there's gentleness too. His lips move against mine and I can taste the rain on his mouth. I'm pressed against the tree, his body is pressed against mine. Just as I think about the bark jabbing my back, I think about his hand on my hip and his other hand in my hair and his lips making their way to my jaw, then my earlobe, my neck, collarbone and back to my lips. His body is hot through our wet clothes and I could stay in this moment forever.

Another boom of thunder follows the lightening and the kiss slows. He pulls his lips from mine, then brings them back in once, twice, three times more. "We should go inside before we're struck by lightning." He takes my hand and we're running through the rain again back to the house.

The wind has scattered all the clothes except one lone sheet that hangs on by a single clothes pin. It whips and twirls in the air and I can't help but feel like the sheet—just barely hanging on, not sure if I know Max, but realizing I'm going to be swept away anyway, so why can't I just let go of the lingering doubt? I feel myself being tugged, ready to let it all go as I watch him run into the house, looking back and flashing his smile that ties me up in knots. He has a past that I have no idea about. But why should that matter to a girl who doesn't even know all of her own secrets?

~~~~

My father was a Nazi. He couldn't have been. I wasn't sure. I had to find out, but could I really just ask him? I still hadn't found the key to the box from the closet. Even if I had, it very well could have nothing of interest to me anyway. It might contain documents for the house or something.

I decided to ask my parents. I was fifteen years old and they couldn't keep me a child forever. It was time to face them.

My father came into the living room, newspaper in hand. "Father?"

"Yes?"

"I need to speak to you. I want to know why we came to America."

He put the paper in his lap and said, "Why? Why, now, does it matter to you?"

"I have these memories. Memories that I can't fit together and that don't make sense."

His eyebrows raised and he said, "Oh? Tell me about these memories."

"Most of them are fuzzy. I remember the boat ride here. How awful it was. I remember being really little and being in some sort of truck. There was a boy. I think his name was Josef. He shared his little blanket with me, the one I have still. I cried for him, but the only thing I remember is seeing his big brown eyes and him handing me the blanket. Then he just kind of disappears from my memories." I paused, waiting for him to say something, but he didn't. His brows furrowed and his face paled.

"I also remember being sick. Was there a time I was very sick?"

Time stood still as the silence grew thicker. I felt I had said something wrong. Slowly, he folded the newspaper and stood, leaving the room. I heard him call for mother to come into the house from the garden. They spoke in hushed tones before coming back in to the living room.

"Gita," my mother said. "I want to speak to you honestly. But I will only tell you these things if you promise to keep them to yourself."

"Who would I tell? I have no one to speak to."

"Fair enough." She took a deep breath before continuing on. "Your father worked for some bad people."

"The Nazis."

They looked at each other, perhaps surprised I had already known.

"I remember his uniform."

My father's turn to speak this time. "Of course you do. Well, we needed to get away from these people. I hated the things they made me do and I wanted to get away. That's why we came to America."

I nodded, taking it in. I was so relieved that he wanted to get away, but it left me with more questions. "I still don't understand why you needed to lie to me about this."

"What we did, leaving, is against the law. We would be killed if we were found. We didn't tell you, because we figured we could move to America, start over, and you would never need to know. Children need to feel safe *and there is no way you would feel safe if you knew. Do you understand why we didn't tell you?"*

"I suppose I do." My mother's eyes brimmed with tears and I didn't want to press any further. I could tell it pained her to speak about. "But we're safe now?"

"Yes, Gita. I don't think anyone even remembers my name. The war has people preoccupied. I can't imagine they would still be looking for me. But that doesn't mean you can be careless. You must never speak of this to anyone. Okay?" Father's eyes, so kind, made me forget the anger I felt at being kept from the truth.

Chapter Thirteen

I watch Max from the kitchen window as he gathers the scattered clothes from the storm. He's soaking wet, so I decide to get some dry clothes from his room and have them in the kitchen ready for him when he comes in.

His room smells like him; masculine and clean, even though it's a little untidy. I get a shirt from the closet and pick up the pair of pants that are slung over the foot of the bed and meet him at the door just as he's coming in. My skin flushes thinking about our kiss in the orchard.

"You mind changing in here so you don't track water through the house?"

"Not at all," he says as he takes the clothes from my hands.

Something falls to the floor and I see it's an envelope. He snatches it from the ground before I can get to it.

"What is that?"

"It's nothing," he answers a little too quickly. "Just a letter."

"Did you get a letter from home?" I give him a chance to tell the truth.

"Yes. Sorry, it's just a little personal." He folds the envelope in half so I can't see the front of it.

My heart sinks and I nod. "I understand. I'll let you get dressed now."

I leave the room thoroughly disappointed. I gave him a chance to tell me the truth and he lied. He must not realize I saw that it was the letter I had written to my aunt. The one I asked him to take the post office earlier today. So why would he have it in his pants still when he told me he had sent it and why did he lie?

~~~~

"So there wasn't any mail for me at the post office yesterday? I'm just worried about my aunt since I haven't heard from her in months. " I ask Max over breakfast the next day.

"No. The mail could be backed up. It happens sometimes. " He sticks the last spoonful of oatmeal in his mouth and stands. "Are you sure you don't want to go with me into town?"

I shake my head. "I'm feeling a little under the weather. Maybe if I lie down for a bit, I'll feel better."

Things are strained between us. I'm sure he senses it. They aren't the same as before I knew he was lying to me. How could they be? But I try my best to fake it. "I'll see you in a bit." I go up to my room and wait to hear the car drive away. As soon as it does, I go to his room. This reminds me of when I knew something was off with my parents and I tried to get into the box. But I just need to find the letter. It is mine after all. It's not like I'm trying to snoop through his personal things and read his mail. I'm still so mad about the whole thing. So mad my heart speeds up as I rifle through his closet. I can't believe he looked me in the eye and told me it was a letter from home when, clearly it wasn't.

I try to replace everything just as it was after I go through his drawers. It's not here. Why would it be? He's probably worried I'll come looking for it and he obviously doesn't want me to find it. Why in the world is he hiding my aunt's letter?

~~~~

I knew there was more to the story. The explanation I got from my parents about why we came to America made sense, I just had a feeling there was a whole lot they weren't saying. So many questions still unanswered. But I didn't want to press too much, hoping if they ever were willing to share information with me again, I needed to tread lightly.

The war was still going on. People were struggling. Somehow we were not. Having the farm helped, but I'd seen my father with money. A lot of it. He kept it in a tin can under a floorboard in the bedroom. We couldn't have made that much from selling eggs and walnuts.

~~~~

"Will you show me your garden?" Max asks.

The summer evening is still warm. The sun is setting in a bath of oranges and pinks and purples. The colors bleed into each other, no clear line of distinction between them all. I love the way the willow bends in the breeze as we walk through the neat rows of plants. I'm still unsettled, not sure how to approach him about my aunt's letter.

"You've been very quiet. Did I do something?" he asks.

"Still not feeling very well is all."

He nods, breaking up a clump of dirt with the toe of his shoe. "Can we speak about the marriage?"

"Okay."

"I don't know about you, but for what it's worth, Gita, I have feelings for you. I thought you did for me as well, but you have been distant the last few days. Can you deny the feelings between us?"

"I will speak honestly as well. I cannot deny the feelings between us. But I'm afraid I'm not quite sure who you are yet, Max. I need time. You need time to show me. I need a husband. One I can trust. We don't have that yet."

His demeanor speaks volumes as his eyes shift to the ground. I know he knows I'm referring to the letter. Yet, he remains silent.

I leave him there in the garden, hoping he tells me soon. I've spent too many years surrounded by secrets and people keeping their lips glued shut. I refuse to live the rest of my life this way.

~~~~

I awoke this morning with the decision to ride to town in hopes of getting some space from the situation. Perhaps that's all I need. I go straight to the post office where I find a one lone piece of mail waiting for me. A bill from the mortuary.

When I get back into the car I slump over, resting my head against the steering wheel, the disappointment of not finding a letter from my aunt overwhelming. I dry my tears, slam the gears into place and take off, resolving in the moment to confront him. Instead of letting my mind run wild and accuse him of something, I will ask him straight out. I'm sick of waiting on other people for truths I have a right to.

Chapter Fourteen

"Why did I used to be called Lidka? I haven't always been Gita, have I?" I was nearly seventeen years old and no longer cared if the questions would upset my parents. I demanded to be told the truth.

Mother sighed. "Why can't you let the past stay where it belongs—in the past? Why must you be such a curious girl?"

"I think I have a right to know where and what I come from. What kind of name is Lidka? Not German?"

"I need to speak to your father before we talk about this. But his heart is weak. If it is too much for him, we will not utter another word about it. Yes?"

"I make no promises." I marched from the room, feeling entitled.

~~~~

I storm into the house and yell, "Max! Where are you?" I make my way through the house and don't see him. Stepping onto the back porch I spot him by the barn. "Max!" I say as I march towards him.

His eyes grow big and he stops mid-swing with the hammer in his hand. "What is it? What's wrong?"

"I demand you speak the truth to me. I have a question for you and if you don't answer me, I will call the police."

His hands go up and he attempts a smile. "Wait. Calm down now. I will tell you what you need to know. Just hold off on calling the police."

"What was that letter you dropped the other day? The one you said was yours, but had my handwriting on it?"

He stiffens slightly and says, "I'll show it to you if it's that important."

I nod and he pulls the letter from his pants pocket, handing it to me with a slight smile. "I'm sorry I didn't tell you the truth. I thought you would be upset that I forgot to mail it. It totally slipped my mind while I was in town."

It's wrinkled from extended handling and it leaves me confused. I glance back at Max who says, "I'm sorry. I shouldn't have lied."

"How did you forget when that's all you went to town for the other day?"

"Because that's not all I went for. I wanted it to be a surprise, but if you want me to tell you, I will."

"Tell me." I need to believe him. Oh, I want him to have a good reason.

"I was looking for a ring. I only have a small amount of money, but I want to give you a proper wedding band, so I was asking around, trying to find a jeweler I could afford." He looks down at his hands as he says, "I don't have any money to my name. I feel I have nothing to give you. You have the land and the house and I come to you with nothing to offer. All I wanted was to give you one thing." The embarrassment in his eyes is genuine. My emotions stir as I look at him and I feel relief for the first time in days.

~~~~

"Why do the Nazis want to kill Jewish people?"

"Because they have been seduced by the devil himself. Many of them started out as great people believing Hitler could make the country better. Then things started happening and his true intention came through."

"But are Jewish people bad?"

Mother shook her head. "Some of the best people I know are Jewish." She leaned down and kissed my head. "Put those ugly things out of your head. Children should not be thinking of such things before going to sleep."

~~~~

I wander out back after seeing him through the window, with two glasses of ice water in hand. I find him sitting in the shade of the barn, his back to me. His hand moves across a notepad and doesn't hear me until I clear my throat. Shutting the notepad he looks up with a smile.

Handing him the glass I slip off my shoes and sit next to him. "Hot, isn't it?"

He nods. "How are you?"

I shrug, not wanting to divulge more. Not ready to tell him how badly I wish I could trust him.

"Are you still mad about the letter? I apologize—"

"No. Don't. You've already said you're sorry and I accept your apology. It isn't that. It's just…"

"What?"

"You have to understand that I have had so many unknowns in my life. My parents kept so many secrets. We didn't talk about anything, so when I feel like you are hiding something from me, it kills me a little inside. I need to find this trust that still isn't there and that kills me because I want it so badly. And for some reason, I'm missing my parents terribly today."

He places a hand on my knee, not saying anything.

Moments tick by as we sip our water. "Would you like a distraction?"

The suggestion takes me off-guard, but I'm surprised when it seems like a good idea so I say yes.

"Want to walk down to the river? It might feel good jumping in."

The thought seems absurd in my current state to just shake off these feelings to go jump in a river. But right now in this moment anything that might numb this pain, take away all the thoughts swirling in my head, seems like a good idea. "Okay. My father had some swim trunks you can wear. Let's go change and get some lunch first."

~~~~

It's late afternoon and I'm trying to cool the house down. It's warmer than usual and sweat is soaking through my dress. The hum of the fan keeps me company in the kitchen. Usually, I open all the windows when I wake up so that by the afternoon it's not as bad, but all had been forgotten until I walked into the house for lunch. I sweat right through my dress and it clings to the small of my back as I prepare ham sandwiches. Max comes in from outside fanning himself with his hat. "I've decided it's too hot to eat indoors today. Let's take our lunch to the river."

After changing into our bathing suits we head down to the river. It's small, but will do. Max runs and jumps in, not realizing how cold it is. When he surfaces with a whoop, his eyes are wide and it makes me laugh, which feels like a betrayal to my mournful mood.

He waves me in but I just sit on the bank and put my feet in. "It's too cold to just jump in."

"That would have been good to know a minute ago." He splashes me, making me squeal.

"Stop!" I splash back, kicking water in his direction but he's already backed up. "I'm not in the mood to play games. I just wanted to come down here to cool off."

His face sombers up before saying, "I know you're trying to process everything, but maybe just having a good laugh will make you feel better for a second. You can always go back to your mood later." He eyes me, gauging my reaction to his words. He must see I find the idea to escape alluring because he says, "Come in!" and starts toward me with a devilish look.

"Don't you dare." I'm just about to jump up to the safety of the bank, when he grabs for my leg. He scoops me up and tosses me in the freezing water. I gasp, hating how it cuts right through me.

But Max doesn't care. He's laughing like he's the funniest thing. "That's for not telling me how cold it was before I jumped in."

I keep my face natural as I walk towards him. I wrap my arms around his neck like I'm going to hug him, but instead push down on his shoulders making him go under.

He comes up with a smile and laughs, grabbing me around the waist. Our faces are so close now and it doesn't take long for one of us to close the gap. The cold fades away because all I can think about is this kiss. It's slow and lovely and sweet and makes me cry. My emotions are too close to the surface to hold back. I wonder if he notices, but then he pulls back, concern etched on his face. His thumbs wipe at my tears. No words needed, everything is said through his actions. He holds me while I cry, letting out all the emotions I've been stowing away.

It's not too long before we are both shivering and need to get out. After drying off I lie down in the sun, letting the heat penetrate the back of my body. It's so relaxing and I'm exhausted. The emotions of the past twenty-four hours and hardly any sleep are catching up with me. Max sits near me, his sketch pad on his lap. I close my eyes as the birds chirp in the tree and the leaves rustle overhead. Knowing how close Max is comforts me and I let myself drift off.

~~~~

I wake to Max rubbing my shoulder. "Gita, you're getting a little red. Should we go in?"

I rub my eyes and roll over, stretching. "How long was I asleep?"

"Forty-five minutes or so."

I nod. "I need to make dinner anyhow."

He carries his pad tucked under his arm and his towel thrown over his shoulder as we make our way to the house. "What did you draw?" I ask.

"It's not ready yet. But when it is, I'll show you." He's quiet and I wonder what he's thinking. We make our way past the barn and are just about to the back lawn when something pierces my foot and I let out a whelp.

"What is it?" Max is at my side where I've stopped and I reach out a hand to steady myself, placing it on his arm.

A nail is sticking out of my foot. It's in fairly deep and I suck in a breath before grabbing it. It's in deeper than I realized and I don't think I can bring myself to pull it out. "Can you help me inside?"

"Do you want to sit down for a minute first?"

I shake my head. "Let's just get in the house." I lean on him as I try to not put my foot down, just hop on my left foot.

Without a word, he picks me up and carries me into the house. "Where are the bandages?" He asks, setting me on the edge of the bathtub.

"The medicine cabinet."

He kneels in front of me taking my foot in his hands and says, "Turn your head."

I want to be tough and am about to protest to tell him I can do it, when the pain intensifies and I do as he says. He tugs the nail out and I can't help but jerk my foot back. He immediately presses a cloth to the bleeding wound and I feel like it's safe to look again.

"You okay?" he asks.

I nod and bite down on my lip, trying to not focus on the pain shooting through my foot. "We need to clean it before putting thc bandage on."

"Take a deep breath," he says as he pours rubbing alcohol over the wound. I close my eyes as he dries the skin, tenderly patting my foot. His hands move slowly, carefully. I watch his face as he works, trying to keep my mind off the pain. After wrapping my foot, he looks up. His eyes are incredibly kind.

"I hope that didn't hurt too much."

"It did, but not because of you."

He smiles. "Don't worry about dinner, I'll figure it out. You rest." He helps me to the couch and hands me a book. "Are you settled for a minute?"

"Yes, thank you."

It's this moment that I realize I love him. Whether I should or not, I do.

~~~~

We are finishing the leftovers Max found in the fridge when I look him square in the eye and say, "Are you still glad you're here?"

His eyes grow large. A beat, a moment to reflect before, "Yes. I am."

My insides sigh. "Good. I am as well." It's the closest I can come to saying I love you without actually saying it.

The funny thing about love, or what I believe is love, is that it doesn't happen when you think it would. Yes, I had feelings for Max when he kissed me so passionately in the orchard. I felt even stronger feelings while star gazing. Everything so romantic. But him sitting across from me at the kitchen table, taking care of me, caring how I feel, showing me he feels something for me—this is when love happens. Everyday life when someone proves to you they care when they don't have to. When someone could leave and they don't. When someone holds you when you're at your worst. There's no reason for me not to trust my gut when it comes to Max. I watch him plating the food, the muscles in his forearms working. His strong hands wipe the rim of the plate where sauce has run down the side and I can't help thinking about that kiss and the way those hands gripped my hips. The thought strikes up a flame in my lower belly. It burns low and slow and I'm just waiting for the moment we kiss again, wondering if I'll be consumed by the flames entirely when it does.

Chapter Fifteen

I jump when I hear him scream. It lasts only a brief moment, so brief I wonder if I imagined it or perhaps it was part of my dream. Lying still, holding my breath I wait for it again. It doesn't come. What do I do? Go to him or act as though I didn't hear it? Reluctantly I get up, put on my bathrobe and enter the hall. I go to knock on his door before I hear soft snores coming from within. Relieved he's okay I make my way back to my bed and lie awake for a while listening to the sound of toads croaking through the open window and wondering what his nightmares are made of.

~~~~

The morning brings bright sun through the curtains that billow out from a soft breeze. I stretch and smile at the sound of Max humming in the kitchen. By the time I make it into the kitchen I smell something burning and Max's humming is replaced by a string of Polish that I assume is cursing.

I fan the smoky air and say, "What happened?"

"I burned the ham. I just stepped out to get some eggs from the coop," he says as he takes the smoking pan to the back porch, "and I guess I was gone too long." He hands me a towel that I use to fan the smoke towards the open window and door.

"I can't believe I did that. Here, let me take that." He reaches for the towel and flaps it wildly.

And then it happens. It's subtle at first and then little by little grabs my stomach, turning it inside out. The smell of smoke, of burning, makes me sick. It triggers a memory buried deep. I choke it down trying to focus on getting the rest of the kitchen aired out, going from the kitchen into the living room opening windows and doors.

When my stomach can't let the memory go, I yell into the kitchen, "I'm going outside for some fresh air."

I hear Max respond but I'm already down the front steps. I take in lungsful of clean, untainted air when it hits me.

A single scene.

I'm on my side, lying in the dirt, face up to the sky and the single stream of smoke coming from the building in the distance. It's mesmerizing and I can't take my eyes off it, but then I smell something burning and suddenly without warning my stomach heaves.

"You okay?" Max's looking at me with concern sketched in his eyes. "You look a little pale."

"My stomach is just upset at the smell is all."

He sits down next to me and rubs light circles against my back. "I'm not so great at cooking."

"You're not kidding." I glance at him from the corner of my eye and he smiles.

"I just wanted to do something nice for you. I'm sorry I burned your breakfast. I could try again."

"No!" I say it a little more forceful than I mean. "I mean I'm not hungry anymore."

"I'll try again. Not today, but I will. I'm really not that bad, promise."

My heart melts a little at the look on his face, loving that he thought of me enough to make me breakfast, even if it didn't quite work out. "Thank you. It was a sweet gesture." Suddenly I feel shy and have to look down.

He leans closer, bumping his shoulder against mine. "Since breakfast is ruined why don't we take a walk? Maybe by the time we get back the house will be aired out." He stands, reaching his hand out to me. The minute I take it my stomach tightens again, but in a good way this time.

"Tell me about Poland," I say as we walk down the gravel lane that leads to the main road. The trees grow thick in patches and then there's stretches with none at all. The summer morning air is sweet and refreshing.

It takes a few moments before he responds. "I don't know that I could ever do it justice. It's home, you know? It's a hard thing to try to tell people about because you want them so badly to feel the same way you do about it, but you know they never will."

"Try." I smile, letting him know he can trust me.

"It's beautiful. Well, it was before the war or what I can remember of it before the war. That's how I choose to remember it now. Beautiful with rolling green hills and a forest we loved to play in as kids. The nearest town had stone streets and old buildings. Everything here seems so new. I like it, but it's not the same as the old stone buildings with so much history, each with their own story. It sounds silly when I say it aloud."

"No. It sounds lovely. You're a bit of a romantic, aren't you?"

The corner of his mouth quirks up. "I guess."

I take his hand and rub my other hand up his arm and lean closer, when my fingers skim a raised scar on the inside of his forearm. He stiffens when my fingers linger. "Does that hurt?"

He shakes his head.

"What's it from?"

"A burn."

"From what?"

He shifts, and although he doesn't, he may as well have pulled away. "The stove."

I examine the rectangular pink smooth skin before he turns his arm away from me.

"We should go to the theater again. Later tonight?"

Even though he smiles, I see through his attempt at changing the subject and decide not to press it. I understand having memories that you would rather forget.

~~~~

"Keep them closed," Max says as he leads me across the lawn.

The afternoon sun slowly turns in the evening sun, settling lower across the field, but I can still feel it on my face. Max picks up his pace and I hold tighter to his hand wondering what this is all about.

When we come to a stop he says, "Okay. Open."

Standing just inside the barn I lay my eyes on a beautiful black walnut bookcase. I steal a glance at Max who smiles and nods for me to go to it. I run my hands along the smooth lines and curves, marveling at its beauty.

"Did you make this?"

"It's my gift to you. Since I haven't much, I thought I would make you something."

"It's just beautiful, Max." I smile, thinking of how wonderful it will look in the living room filled with my father's books.

"Shall we bring it inside? I might need a little help. It's heavy."

After some maneuvering, we get it in just the right spot next to the window. "Thank you so much. It's the most beautiful gift anyone has ever given me." I wrap my arms around his waist as he pushes the hair off my shoulders and looks in my eyes. The intensity from his eyes settles into me, down to my bones. I can't break the gaze and wait a breath before he kisses me and heaven help me if I don't float a foot off the ground.

Chapter Sixteen

Max is in town picking up a few things while I clean the house. I have the records playing, windows open and can't help but feel better than I've felt in my life. Just a few short months ago I felt like a girl, naïve to the world, but Max makes me feel like a woman. There's something about the way he holds me when we dance and looks at me or catches my waist as he passes me in the kitchen.

I move to the bookcase he made for me and pull the first row of books down to dust when an envelope falls to the floor. Curious, I pick it up and pluck out the paper inside.

Her lips speak words I want to kiss from her lips. Her skin, creamy and smooth, beckon my fingertips to leave a trail of memories across the silky plains of her back. The furrow in her brow calls to my soul which longs to sooth her, calm her.

Her eyes. More golden in the afternoon sun, speak to me in a way any spoken language would completely and utterly fail. She sees through me and into me with her hazel eyes.

I'm a drifter, a roamer. I belong nowhere and everywhere. But she makes me want to stop; to dig my heels into the ground and stay. With her. Always running, being someone else and she makes me believe I don't have to. That what I've done in the past will just disappear if I stay; vaporize like the dew under the heat of a burning sun. No longer running, pretending. She stills my anxious soul.

A poet she makes me. A lover, a romantic, a school boy, a man.

My wandering heart did not count on this. To love. It screams at me to leave her, move on while I can. But my heart proves stronger for the moment. I now see why love drives men to war, murder, madness. It's stronger than common sense, this love. Stronger than the pull of the moon. It leaves me weak. Yet, I have no desire to resist any longer.

And I have yet to even kiss her.

My face heats as I read it over again wondering if Max wrote this and meant for me to find it. Is it even Max's? Could it have been stuck in the pages of my Father's books and I not noticed it before? I go through the rest of the books, shaking them to see if there are any more of these mysterious letters.

Then I read it over again. The words sink in and shake something up inside of me, move me. Suddenly the room is too hot and I go to the refrigerator for a cold drink. I decide to keep it and wait to see if he says anything about it.

He doesn't.

The letter stays next to the scrap of blanket under my pillow. I pull it out every night and read it, wanting it to be about me. The thought of Max writing these things makes my heart stutter. I toy with the idea of writing something back but I'm too much of a coward. I pull out my own journal, the one I've been writing to my parents in and decide it's a safer place to speak to him. I hesitate at first, and then just write.

> *Love*
> *You. Me. Strangers no more.*
> *Scared*
> *To be lonely, vulnerable, a wife*
> *Reassured*
> *By your eyes, your words, your touch*
> *Anticipating*
> *The night, the day after, forever*

~~~~

It felt like forever since I'd eaten. Or been hugged. The heavy feeling weighed me down until I wanted to just stay there. The dirt didn't seem so uncomfortable anymore. I wanted it to be over. Whatever it was. It just felt like eternity and there was an absence of hope or comfort. 'Just let it be over,' I thought. 'Does anyone

know I'm here? Where are my parents?' I remember
thinking that maybe if I lie there long enough everyone
would stop seeing me if they hadn't already. It felt like
I'd been there forever. And forever is not a good feeling
when there is no hope to be felt.

~~~~

The county fair. I've never been but always wanted to
go. We drove past it once when I was younger and as we
passed by I hung my head out the open window. It
looked like the people there were having more fun than I
had ever had in my whole young life. But we couldn't
stop. My parents didn't see it the same way I did. So
when I heard on the radio that it was happening this
weekend I declared to Max that we were going.

The smell of desserts and treats drape the late
summer evening air with a heavy sweetness as we make
our way to the ticket booth. I haven't been in a crowd of
people for years and it isn't as scary as I thought it
would be. More than anything, it energizes me. All our
excitement melding together, feeding off of one another.

"What first?" Max's hand is in mine as we pass the
popcorn stand. He looks especially handsome tonight
with his sleeves rolled up, his hat atop his combed back
dark hair. He's tan from working outside all summer and
I feel an unusual amount of pride holding his hand in
front of all these people.

"That," I say pointing to the Ferris wheel.

"That it is." His smile is the most genuine smile I have ever witnessed. Such joy in it you can't help but feel it yourself.

We step onto the swaying cart after handing a man our ticket and settle into the seat. "How safe do you think this is?" I ask. "It feels a little rickety."

"Just sit back and relax, you'll love it."

The evening is nearly gone, making way for the night and the lights throughout the fairgrounds that speed by us, blurring into streams of color as the Ferris wheel goes around. The feeling of my stomach dropping makes me giggle.

I look over at Max who grins at me.

"This is the most free I've ever felt," I say as the wind whips my curly hair around. Instead of waiting for Max to lean in, I take the opportunity and kiss him on top of the Ferris wheel with the wind on my skin and I wonder how I lived without all this before.

After stopping at nearly all the rides and funhouse and sampling popcorn, hot dogs and a caramel apple, we end up at the dance floor. The band is playing and Max doesn't miss a beat before taking my hand and spinning me around, then dipping me. When the music slows he brings me in closer. Leaning my head on his chest, him leaning his chin on the top of my head, I feel like crying because I'm so happy.

"This is incredible." He tips my head up to look at him. "You're incredible." Just as I think he's going to press his lips to mine, he spins me out and then back to him. We stay that way until the last song is played.

Driving home the music is on low, conversation nonexistent, but contented silence fills the car. We're several miles from home when Max suddenly drives off the road right into a field filled with tall grass.

"What are you doing?" I grab hold of the door handle as the car bumps over the uneven ground then jolts to a stop. He's still not the best driver.

"Taking a detour." He hops out of the car and runs around to my door, opening it and offering me his hand. Once out of the car he says, "Just look at the sky. Can you believe the stars tonight?" The stars and moon are bright tonight, lending us their light.

He stretches out his arms and spins around before looking at me. "Come. If you spin just right, it looks as though the stars bleed together creating these streaks of lights."

I shake my head. "You're crazy."

"Just try it!" He spins faster and I roll my eyes before joining him.

"We look like crazy people," I say, still spinning.

"But happy crazy people." He trips and falls to the ground and I can't help but laugh and collapse next to him, too dizzy to keep going.

We look up into the sky as we lay on our backs, trying to catch our breath and stop our heads from spinning. Moments go by before he finds my hand in the dark. "Do you ever wonder about the people on the other side of the stars?" His voice is quiet, reverent almost.

"What do you mean?"

"I just figure that's where heaven is. On the other side of the stars. And I wonder sometimes about the people there and what they do and what it looks like. And if it holds all the people that have ever died, is it hard to find someone they want to find?"

I watch his profile as he speaks and even in the little light we have I can see the pain in his eyes. "I guess I haven't thought about it that way before. But I like to think my parents are there together." Moments pass as I wonder who he thinks about. "I like that: the other side of the stars."

The corner of his mouth turns up as he turns to look at me. Then he puts his lips against mine, tender and slow with a near painful emotion seeping from him.

When he pulls away I ask, "Did you have any girlfriends in Poland?"

"Many."

I pull back to get a look at his face and when I see his smile I realize he's joking. I slap his chest, but he pulls me in tighter, wrapping his arms around me, laughing.

"How do you feel about me? I feel like I know, but I want to hear it in words from you."

"You want to know how I feel about you?" He pauses, not as if he needs to think about it, but to make sure he has my full attention. When he speaks again, his words are hushed, yet thick with assurance. "Have you ever seen storm clouds roll in? It's like that, but in fast motion; beautiful in a frightening way. Knowing that a fury of a storm is coming, but you want it as much as you don't. Or maybe it's more like the ocean when you get caught on the underbelly of a wave. The rise and fall and swirling madness, being tossed about like a ragdoll. It's being swept up in a force that you have no power against, but it's thrilling at the same time; makes you feel alive. That's how I feel about you." He moves closer. "When I look at you and you see me. When we touch." He's a breath away. "The feeling of falling in love is real and frightening and painfully beautiful."

His finger traces over my top lip and it makes me shiver. "How do you feel about me?" he asks.

"My words wouldn't do it justice. I'm not sure I can explain."

"Then show me," he whispers against the skin of my neck.

And I do.

~~~~

The next day I pen my feelings in a letter to Max, hoping I can express my feelings adequately because I'm still too shy to say these things in person.

Every time I take a breath I worry I'll fall apart. Exhale too hard and I'll shatter. Inhale too deeply and I'll implode. My pain is a splinter on a pane of glass waiting for the slightest increase in pressure to be its undoing.

Breathe on me and let me feel your life. Breathe and perhaps if I match my breath to yours I won't cross that line of self-destruction. Give me a sign, a reason to keep myself whole. Look at me with eyes that tell me you want to be here. With me. Only me. Make me enough.

Your eyes open and I know it's over. Because as hard as I try, there will be no controlling my breathing. I know in this moment that you will put your lips on mine and I want it to happen as much as I don't and I'm scared. This moment before we take that step. You give me the slightest touch on my hand from yours. More of a brushing, but every one of those hundreds of pores feel it. I hold my breath now as your eyes fall on my mouth then travel back to my eyes. And when you speak, my heart trips and I'm still holding my breath, controlling it, keeping myself together. But as soon as I realize what you've said I struggle.

"This is what love feels like, no?" Your voice is a reverent whisper that reaches further than my ears.

I test my voice. "I believe so."

You trail your finger to catch a piece of hair that rests on my cheek and you wrap it around your finger before laying it back down. And you keep it there; you let your finger fall to my neck and your thumb skims over my collarbone. There's no hope of keeping my breathing in check because you steal it away. Your lips press against mine tenderly and I feel like weeping for I never knew what it would feel like to have my breath taken. Too worried I was with finding the balance between too hard and too soft I hadn't given much thought to what it would be like if you took over completely and somehow the pain begins to ebb. It begins to dissipate like the spoonful of sugar you had put in your iced tea, the very sugar I can taste now.

Words will never be needed between us again because what is being said with the way you hold me right now will last far longer than any whispered sentiments.

Your lips find my ear as you say, "Will you be my wife?"

I know what you're asking. And it's not about the piece of paper we had signed over a month ago.

I nod and I see surprise flash across your face before you bring your lips back to mine.

And then I shatter. And it's more magnificent that I ever imagined it could be.

~~~~

Chapter Seventeen

The next night we're in the kitchen, radio on like it always is in the evenings, the windows are open letting the cooler night air blow through and Max is helping me with dinner.

"Ow." He yanks his hand back from the stove and rushes to the sink.

"Did you burn your hand?"

He nods and I go to him, turning his hand over so I can see the angry stripe of red across three of his fingers. I suck in a breath because it hurts just looking at it. "You got it right across your fingertips. Hold it under the water and I'll see if I have any ointment for it."

When I return from the bathroom, burn ointment in my hand, he's bent over the sink, his forearms leaning against the front edge of it, fingers under the stream of water. "Here. My mother said this is the best thing for burns. Let me see your hand."

He sets his hand palm up in mine. "This is a pretty bad burn." There are blisters already beginning to form and I hope I'm helping more than hurting him as I spread the balm on as gingerly as I can.

"Ouch." He flinches.

"Hold still. You move and it will make it worse."

"Are you sure this will help? It's not feeling better. Maybe I should keep it under the water for a bit longer." He jerks his hand back as I rub some more of the ointment on the burn.

"It takes a while for it to work. It's not magic. I'm almost done, just hold still." I can feel his eyes on me as I work to wrap a bandage around his finger. When I finish, I wipe my own fingers on a dish towel.

"Thank you. You are very good at that. You should be a nurse." He smiles and I realize he's joking, so I slap his shoulder.

"Stop it. You are such a tease. You'll thank me later when it feels better. Just no rinsing it off."

"Yes, ma'am."

His laugh lingers as I take the things back to the medicine cabinet in the bathroom. I'm not gone more than two minutes when I hear the kitchen sink turn on, knowing he's rinsing his hand off.

While dinner cooks I get the book I've been reading from my nightstand and take it into the living room. I poke my head in the kitchen as I pass by. "You okay in here?"

He nods, "It will be done soon. I've got it."

I look pointedly at his unwrapped hand and he just waves me off. "You'll be sorry when it starts hurting again," I say.

I open my book after sinking into the sofa and find an envelope. My heart pounds as I open it and see the same handwriting as the first letter I found in the bookcase.

Past Lovers

Everything they were:

Skin, lips, tangled hair

All surface

Flesh, but no soul

Racing pulse, but no heart

Wanting, but no needing

Empty whispers caught up in a frenzied heat

A fleeting moment

Empty feelings

Nothing

You:

Flesh and soul and racing heart

Wanting and needing, craving, fullness

Joy encompassing

Passion

Substance

Torment and contentment

Promises real and true and never to be broken

An eternity

Everything they were and everything they were not

Everything

Book forgotten, I walk to Max in the kitchen, turn off the burner, and say to him, "Let's move you into my room tonight."

~~~~

Waking up with him is an indescribable feeling. I'm so full of joy, my chest feels like it will burst. Lying in his arms, our hands intertwined, he says, "Aren't hands amazing?"

"How so?"

"I don't know, all the things they do. They can hold a lover's hand, their body."

Heat creeps up my neck as he continues.

"Our hands are usually the first thing we use to connect with another human by shaking hands. I guess the whole body is pretty fascinating. It's like our bodies connect with our souls both letting us know when we like something." He shakes his head. "I can't really explain it. Like when I run my finger up your arm and it raises goose bumps." My arms follow his instructions and bumps pop up across my body. "Your body responds to my body, knowing that it likes it. And when our bodies are even closer don't you ever feel that connection? Something more than physical? An emotional connection that we call love. It has to be the body and soul connecting."

"You are such a romantic." He lifts my hand to his mouth as he presses a kiss against my fingertips. He reluctantly gets out of bed and gets dressed and something about him putting his shirt on is so incredibly appealing and sexy. He sees me noticing and can't help but grin.

"I need to go into town to pick up more nails for the fence. Anything you need?"

"Could you just drop my letter off at the post office? I still haven't heard from my aunt and I can't help but worry."

"I'm sure she's fine, but I'd be happy to." With a kiss on my forehead he leaves.

"It's on the kitchen counter," I holler after him.

It takes me a long while to get out of bed, being so happy and not in a hurry to do much today. I draw a bath and take my time getting ready. Just as I slip my dress over my head I hear the car come down the lane and smile at the thought of Max being home so soon.

A knock at the door makes me jump. Why is he knocking? I round the corner to the front door and see a man I don't know standing on the other side of the screen door.

Approaching the door the man removes his hat and says, "Miss. I'm looking for the daughter of Karl Wagner." His German accent is thick, but he knows English well.

My heart thumps hard in my chest feeling so caught off guard. "I am."

He smiles as though he's relieved. "It's nice to meet you. I believe your aunt wrote to you letting you know I'd be coming."

My brows furrow wondering what he could be talking about. "I'm sorry, I'm not sure what you're referring to."

"I'm sure she wrote you. I know I'm quite late, but I had an unfortunate…incident." He motions to his arm which until now I hadn't noticed is in a sling.

"I still don't understand…" I shake my head. "Who are you?"

"Pardon me, Miss. I'm Max Roth. Your aunt sent me here to see about marrying you."

LEO
Poland

Chapter Eighteen

I was eleven when we were taken to the Ghetto. A boy with no real understanding of what was happening in the small Polish town where I lived, let alone in the rest of the world. My home had always seemed safe until the day the men with the uniforms came and took us all away.

We went to a larger city that was full of other Jews. We were told what we could and could not do. I was no longer able to go to school. Father could no longer work at the bank. Even though we were scared, my parents always kept our minds busy and said we were on an adventure of some sort. Even though I was only eleven, I realized it was a meager attempt at distraction.

I was happy to see so many of our neighbors there as well. My best friend, Albert, and I kept each other company and ran around together. We never spoke of our homes we left or the school teacher we disliked or the path through the woods we made with our bicycles.

We played silly games and teased the girls our age and acted as though this was normal, this Ghetto. Within a year or so I was also well versed in distraction.

Then history repeated itself.

We were together at first. My mother, Halina, my father, Moshe, and little sisters Ania and Cyryl. All of us were rounded up and forced to march to the train yard. They gave us only a few minutes to gather our things. My father had one suitcase and my mother another. When I look back on that day I think of the silly things we wanted to bring. My sister Cyryl cried for her new doll. She had just turned four the week before and hadn't been without it since. At the last moment Father said she could take it if she carried it the whole way because there was no more room in the suitcases. He did it just to quiet her. My mother grabbed her jewelry she had gotten from her mother and rolled it carefully inside one of her dresses, worried it would get broken on the journey.

Ania was nine years old and wanted nothing except her books. She was a gifted reader and unlike a lot of girls her age, didn't want to play. She wanted to read. So the thought of leaving her books behind sent tears down her face. Books were heavy. She was allowed to take only one.

I would have brought my bicycle had there been a choice, but it was back home. And since there was nothing else I really wanted to bring, I stuffed a satchel of hard candies into the suitcase. I had kept them since we had first been taken. Only sucking on one for a minute or two every month, trying to make them last. There was hardly any food, let alone candy in the Ghetto.

On our way to the train station our group grew bigger with each house we passed. The men draped in guns went into houses, pulling people out, yelling or shoving if they moved too slowly. My friend, Albert, soon joined us and suddenly it was a relief. Wherever we were going at least I'd have Albert to play with. He was further back in the crowd and when he saw me, I gave a small wave. His eyes wide, glanced around before slightly lifting his fingers. I guess nervous about drawing attention to himself.

I tried to keep my mind off of how terrified I was. Because I was. Everyone was. Some must have known where we were going. Others, like myself, had no idea and somehow that seemed worse to me than knowing. To keep my mind off the guns and the dogs I counted the stars on the coats of the others. The ones we had been wearing for a while to let others know we were Jews. I turned around, walking backwards so I could see them, and counted until my father told me to turn back around. Soon it was all I saw; stars marching to the trains.

Once we arrived we stood there facing the trains, hesitant to go in, and that's when the panic set in. We didn't have too much time to think about it as we were shoved and prodded into the cars until they were full. So full was our car that we had to raise our arms above our heads in order to fit in. There was barely enough room to stand, let alone sit. One of the men with the guns shoved a bucket into the chest of the man next to me, stating it was where we were to relieve ourselves. The doors slid shut, the darkness set in, and to my disappointment the stars didn't shine.

My family huddled together, clinging to each other in the darkness as the trained hissed to life and chuffed down the tracks. Most of us stayed quiet, others did not. Mothers cried over their children. Children cried because they were tired and wanted to lie down. We soon figured out that if we stood front to back we were allowed a bit more room to move and breath, which was another problem. The air was so thick with no ventilation and so many bodies. The occasional sliver of air we got through the crack in the sides of the car was a gift.

We rode all night into the next day and into the next night. By then we were hungry and thirsty. The train would stop sometimes and every time we waited for the doors to slide open. They didn't. We figured we were picking up more people.

That second night someone had worked a slat off the tiny barred window and was able to stick their hand out to catch the falling snow. Soon there was a collective shoving to get to it, each eager to quench our thirst. When it was my father's turn, he stuck his hand out and brought it back in, covered in snow. My mother pushed it away when he offered it to her first, saying, "The children."

We scraped the snow from his palm and licked at it. He did this several times and it wasn't enough, but our turn was over.

We ended up in the corner of the car, huddled together again. I rested against my mother who had her arms around me. "Where are they taking us?" I said it so quietly I wasn't sure she heard me.

"I don't know," she said.

Looking back, I believe this is what frightened me most, the fact that my parents didn't know where we were going. That it was out of their hands. They were supposed to be in charge and suddenly someone else was. It was unsettling as a child to have someone in charge of your parents.

That second night after the snow had stopped and people were no longer trying to get to the window, a sort of despair fell upon us. We didn't know how long we would be in the cattle cars and we didn't know where they were taking us. Children, including Ania and Cyryl cried, begging for food. We were all tired, our bodies fatigued and weak from standing for so long. The little ones and the elderly took turns on the floor while people had to stand over them, straddling their legs.

The smell from the relief bucket made my stomach turn. The bucket was passed around as needed and I was always relieved when it would go away from us. There were only a couple of babies in our car, but both had run out of clean cloths for diapers. We had no way of disposing of the waste. One failed attempt at dumping it through the crack in the window cured us of trying it again.

One woman, a mother with a baby in her arms, cried and cried along with her baby. I covered my ears because I couldn't stand the way it sounded. I hated the way it made me feel hearing everyone's cries. Helpless. I was completely helpless.

At some point I fell asleep and woke to someone speaking. For the most part, the train car was quiet. He was saying Tehillim. More voices joined in and it brought me comfort hearing my father's voice repeating words I had heard hundreds of times before. The beauty of the words did not escape me and for the first time I heard, truly heard the words of the prayer. It was the first time I remember being moved by words.

Chapter Nineteen

Early on the third day, the train came to a stop. It stayed stopped and we were all quiet, listening to hear what was going on. Some pressed up against the small opening of the window, straining to see anything.

"I think they are unloading," a man said from the window.

The few people who were on the floor, scrambled up and we all faced the door, waiting for our turn. There was a click and the doors slid open, letting in a brightness we hadn't seen in a few days. We squinted as they yelled at us, "Beeile dich!" Hurry up!

We piled out of the car to a place we didn't recognize, stretching our limbs. An older man stumbled on his step off the train and fell to the dirt. People rushed to him, aiding him to his feet before the men in the uniforms saw him.

"Leave your things where they are," they said.

My father didn't hesitate at all before setting down the suitcases.

"Ausrichten!" They kept yelling. "Austrichten!"

I hurried after my father who carried Ania. "Where are we going?"

He kept his voice low and said, "They are telling us to line up. Hurry. Just do as they say."

My mother and Cyryl and I kept right behind him as we lined up with the others, still confused as to what was going on.

We were surrounded by the men in guns and uniforms. A few of which had big dogs that strained against their leashes. They were mean-looking dogs that bared their teeth when someone would get too close. We stood in a line that I couldn't see the front of. I didn't know what we could possibly be standing in line for. But inch by inch we moved closer to a group of men yelling, "Recht! Link!" That's all they said.

As we drew nearer I saw they were separating the people into two different lines. My mother grabbed my father's coat. "What are they doing?"

He shook his head and slipped his arm around her shoulders, pulling her close. She trembled as we stepped forward. Only two people in front of us before we reached the men.

Just as those two people were appointed their proper line my father turned to me and whispered, "Tell them you're fifteen years old. Understand? Fifteen."

I nodded as we stepped forward. One of the men assessed my mother and said, "Link!" and pointed to the line at our left. Immediately he said to my father, "Recht!" pointing to the right.

My mother's eyes brimmed with fear. She shook her head ever so slightly looking into my father's eyes, but he just nodded, telling her to do what she was asked. "We are just being separated into men and women, I'm sure." He tried to reassure her.

She moved to hug him, but the guard shoved in between them, ripping Ania out of my father's arms. Ania cried when the man plucked her from my father, because she was terribly afraid of strangers. Mother grabbed her from the man and Cyryl followed. She glanced at me, hesitating until another one of the men yelled at her to keep moving.

They shoved my father in the direction they had ordered him and then I stood there alone in front of a man who asked, "Age?"

My father's words came back to me, slapping me out of my shock at seeing my mother and sisters taken. "Fifteen."

He looked me up and down then nodded and shouted, "Recht!"

I ran to catch up with my father who I embraced fiercely. He allowed it only a moment before pushing me away saying, "We must not let them know we are together. I fear they will split us up if they do."

He turned me around so I was in front of him with my eyes on the back of the head in front of me.

I strained to see my mother and sisters until I spotted them. My mother's eyes were already on me. She mouthed something to me, but the distance was too great between us. All I could really tell was all three of them were crying.

I glanced back at my father whose own eyes brimmed with tears and realized I may never see them again. There was no other reason I could think of that would make my father cry.

We waited for what seemed like thirty minutes or so and then they told us to march. People strained, looking around for loved ones as we went through the gates. Just when I thought I wouldn't be able to see them, I saw my mother again. Reaching towards me. The pain and the ache that filled my chest at that moment lies within me still. I cried out for her when her face got lost in the crowd of people. In a moment of panic, I took off, planning on reaching her.

My father grabbed me and covered my mouth. His frenzied voice saying, "You mustn't cry. She's not here. We'll see her soon, but only if you're good. If you're a not good boy, they won't let us see her again." His eyes wide with fear, darted around. The panic I saw in him stilled me some and I tried my hardest to stop.

They pushed and shoved us as people yelled and others cried out for loved ones. The agony of that moment is burned in my memory. It's a feeling that I can still recall, still feel when I think about it.

As we were being led through a large gate a man shoved me aside, trying to get through the crowd. "Halt!" a man in uniform yelled. The man didn't. He had a star sewed on his coat like Papa and I both did. The uniform man yelled for him to stop again just as another man in uniform closer to us grabbed the man and struck him down with his stick. He kept hitting, striking him over and over. Everyone backed up, leaving a circle of space for the man to fall. Papa turned me around and said, "Don't look."

"Help him, Papa."

"I can't. I'm sorry, son, but I can't."

"Stop them. They're hurting him!" I cried into his shirt.

"You'll understand one day why I can't. Maybe if I had nothing to lose I would step in, but I have you."

At first I thought he was somehow blaming me. Now it's very clear why he couldn't intervene.

Panic has a feel to it. Nearly tangible. It snatches you up in a vice grip and shakes you until you feel it and breathe it and produce more panic, spreading it around. It's an incredibly powerful emotion. I think that's why the men in uniform ordered us to keep moving. A bunch of panicked people would be hard to control. We stepped over and around the man who lay in a heap in the dirt and even though I wasn't supposed to, I reached out and clenched my father's hand in mine. He squeezed back almost too hard, but I didn't complain.

Chapter Twenty

We were taken to a building where the SS guard told us to undress and leave our clothes and shoes. Father didn't hesitate, so I followed him and stripped down like the rest of the men. There was nothing to cover ourselves with, even though I tried with my hands the best I could. I couldn't bring myself to look at anyone except my father who kept his eyes straight ahead.

"Take this to the barber," said the guard as he handed me a card with a number on it.

I so badly wanted to speak to my father, to hear his voice reassure me, but I didn't want to take the chance of getting caught. We were brought into another room where we stood in another line. I watched as the first man was shaved of all his body hair, but kept my eyes on the ground after that. I knew the men were humiliated enough having to go through it, without me adding to the disgrace. My father went first and still my eyes stayed on the ground until a voice boomed, "Nächster."

It was my turn. I chanced a glance towards the door at the end of the room, but my father was not there. The pit in my stomach grew, so I kept telling myself I was right behind him. I couldn't see him at the moment, but I would soon.

The cold steel of the razor touched my scalp and I closed my eyes, telling myself I was okay. "You are okay, Leo. Take a deep breath. Think of something else. Somewhere else." I repeated it as the barber worked his way down my body. Until the shaving was over. I kept repeating it as they rubbed stinging disinfectant into the newly shaved ski and until I was pointed through the door.

Not knowing what came next was perhaps the worst thing about that day. About all the days that followed. The places your mind wandered were many times worse than reality. But more often than not, reality was worse than your imagination.

I joined a group of men and as we waited our group grew in size, all of us trying to not to touch each other as we waited for our next command. I caught sight of my father and I went to work my way to him, but he shook his head. My heart sank remembering him saying it was best if they didn't know we were together.

"Folgen!" Follow, the guard said. He took us into a large room with shower heads lining the walls and instructed us to wash under the showers already running with frigid cold water. As soon as the stream hit my chest I cringed and gasped for air. The sharp cold made it hard to breathe. I washed as quickly as I could but not before the water numbed my skin. Shivering, we were then finally given something to cover ourselves with;

long underwear, a striped shirt and pants and a cap. Each of us dressed quickly as the guards shouted to hurry.

I thought we were done. I wanted so badly to be done. I hoped that now that we were showered and dressed we would be taken to our families. But I was wrong.

We were given a form to fill out asking our names and birthdates and addresses. This is where we were given a number—each of us a different one—which was etched into our skin with a needle and ink. I went away. Let my mind fly me up out of the building and back to my home. It wasn't so much the pain as it was the uncertainty that I needed to escape. When I opened my eyes after it was over I went wherever they directed me in a sort of haze. It had been several days since I slept properly. I was scared. I was uncertain. And worst of all, I was alone.

~~~~

As luck would have it, my father and I ended up in the same block in quarantine while they made sure we didn't carry any diseases we could infect the rest of the camp with. We were crammed into a long room that housed wooden bunks which ran the length of the walls, three tall. The wooden slats that made up the bunks had nothing except one blanket per bed which we were expected to sleep two or three men in each one. It was the size of my bed back home and I wondered how they expected three grown men to fit.

Father kept me at a distance, though I could feel him watch me often. I knew he didn't want to draw attention to us, but my loneliness peaked when I could see him, but not be with him. There were four men separating us on the top row of beds. But it may as well have been four miles.

That night when darkness consumed the bunkhouse and I was sure no one could see me, I cried. I had held it in all day and I just couldn't do it any longer. I hoped Papa didn't know it was me. I was afraid he would tell me to be quiet and that I wasn't being brave like he told me to be. There were others crying as well and I soon realized one of them was him. My two sisters, my mama, my best friend, Albert; people who were a part of my life since I could remember, gone. Just...gone. I cried myself to sleep for all the people I missed.

～～～～

Sometime in the night I woke to my father shaking my shoulder. Somehow he had slipped between me and the man next to me.

"I'm not sure when we will be able to speak, so I wanted to ask if you are okay." He kept his voice a soft whisper.

"How can I be, Tata? I'm scared."

"I'm not sure." I suppose it was my calling him daddy for the first time since I was a small child that made his voice crack. It took a minute before he went on. "Whatever you do, don't get separated from me. Do you understand? We must keep an eye on each other, but not let them know we are together. But we stick together. Yes?"

I nodded and after a much-too-brief embrace, he went back to his spot.

~~~~

The second day was perhaps the day I realized we were there to stay.

Early in the morning, before the sun rose, a gong sounded from outside our door and the Blockfuhrer rushed in, barking orders for us to get up. That morning and throughout the day the rules and expectations were drilled into us relentlessly. Stand here, count off, fold your blanket like this, piss now, say this, go there, move faster, don't speak, speak up! I moved quickly, paying attention to what they wanted as to not draw attention to myself.

They taught us German words and phrases so we knew the commands that were screamed at us each day. We were made to sing German songs and learn how to properly fold our blankets. We were issued a single bowl that we were to hold onto because this was not only what held our food, but also our urine at night since we were not allowed to go to the latrine after lights out.

The food was something I would expect a pig to turn his nose up to, but by the fourth day of not eating, you choke it down. We were allowed watered down coffee in the morning, a measly helping of nasty soup at midday and in the evening a chunk of bread. If we were lucky we would have something else with it like a touch of marmalade or cheese.

It was because of the food I suspect, that a lot of men got sick. Since we were unable to go to the bathroom at night, we were given a bucket which overflowed often. With little to no ventilation, the air was unbearable with the amount of bodies crammed into such a small space. If I thought the undressing and showering in groups was degrading, it had nothing on the living conditions.

Eventually our time in Quarantine expired when they deemed us all healthy enough to not pose a threat to the rest of the camp.

"Line up, single file. Men on one side. Boys on the other."

I looked up at Papa, slipping my hand into his, squeezing tight. He looked at me and whispered, "You do everything they tell you. I will find you soon. We won't be apart for long. Remember, be a good boy so you can go home."

I nodded, but fear writhed in my belly, scaring me enough to fill my eyes with tears.

"Be a good boy."

Then Papa let go of my hand.

Chapter Twenty-One

I was put to work in a field with several other men and older boys. We cleared the field, removing rocks and any other debris. It was hard, exhausting work that left me sore each night. It wasn't long before my hands cracked and bled from the sheer amount of rock I moved. As bad as my body felt from the strenuous labor, it paled in comparison to my hunger pains. Too much work on too little food to sustain us.

Back home even when we were poor, struggling to find food, we had enough to fill our bellies. My father was a banker, but had lost his job. It wasn't until recently I learned he was forced to hand over his business. At the time neither he nor my mother spoke of why he was forced from his job and why we were forced to where yellow stars in public. Or why suddenly I could no longer attend school.

While I worked I daydreamed about Mother and my sisters. Ania and Cyryl pestered me from sun up to sun down and I tried to get away from them on a daily basis. Now, I would do anything to see again. If I thought about Mother too much I would cry, so I tried not to. But sometimes my mind wandered and I thought about food that she would make, which would then make me hungrier. I would attempt to turn my thoughts to my best friend and how we would play in the fields after we did our chores. We were so much alike. He was an only child and like a brother to me. I missed him. I ached for all of them. The gone.

Before coming here I had of course heard of the Nazis; knew they had something, if not everything, to do with all the changes in our lives, but it still didn't make sense. The scariest part was not knowing when I was going to go home. I just wanted to know where my parents were and when I would get to sleep in my own bed and have Mama feed me. It sounds like I was a baby, but I felt no shame in longing for my mother. The loneliness was overwhelming.

Then, on the twelfth day, I saw Papa. He was brought to the field where I worked. I dropped the large rock I held and ran to him, throwing my arms around his waist.

He held onto me and took my face in his hands, searching. "Are you okay?"

I studied his face as well. He was dirty, but otherwise looked okay.

I nodded, not able to speak because of the emotion choking off the words. "Good. You've been a good boy. Go back to work, quick before they see you and we'll meet up soon. I promise." He kissed my head and said, "Go, my boy."

I went back reluctantly, but still looked over at him from time to time. He kept his head down, doing what he had been ordered to do, so I decided to do the same. Twice while I was looking he met my eyes and winked. The relief of seeing him, knowing he was close, made sleep come a little better that night.

~~~~

The boy called Alfred slept next to me on the top bunk. We were piled three high in rows that filled up the room on nothing but wooden slats that were our beds, just like in quarantine. He had been silent for the whole week as had I until he spoke one night in the dark. "What's your name?"

I wasn't sure who he was speaking to as I couldn't see in the blackness of the night. He repeated himself before I realized he must be speaking to me.

"My name is Leo."

It was quiet for several minutes and I wondered if he had heard me.

Then a small voice. "Are you scared, Leo?"

The simple question made me want to cry. "Very."

"Me too." His voice was barely a whisper that nearly got swallowed up in the darkness.

That was all that was said. In the morning I paid more attention to the boy, who was smaller than I, perhaps nine or ten years old. He was the youngest of the boys that I could see. He stuck close to me and silently followed me. We sat next to each other when we

ate and he watched everything I did. It would have
bothered me normally. But my life was anything but
normal and I liked him. He reminded me of my best
friend whom I missed and wondered where he was. The
boy didn't speak all that day, but when night fell and
most the room was quiet I heard his small voice again,
"Did they take your family too?"

"Yes," I said.

"Do you know where they took them?"

"My papa is here, but I don't know where they took
my mother and sisters."

"My papa isn't here. He came with me, but I
haven't seen him since the first day."

I considered what he said before saying, "I'm sure
he's here. I bet they have him working somewhere we
can't see. From what I've seen, it's a big place."

"He was worried they would not let him stay
because of his leg. It was broken and he couldn't really
walk on it. I heard him talking to a man on the train
when they thought I was asleep and he said he was
worried about what they would do with men who
couldn't work." A few moments passed before he added.
"Leo, do you know what they do with men who can't
work? Where do they send them?"

My stomach dropped. I didn't know, but I had seen
the way they treated men who were working too slowly.
Some they killed without hesitation and I'm sure the boy
had witnessed it too. Then others simply disappeared. "I

bet they send them to the hospital to get better. I bet he'll be back very soon."

The boy stayed silent and I hoped if nothing else, he'd find comfort in my lie.

~~~~

A month in, I had lost weight and my hip bones were sticking out. The clothes they gave me when I first arrived were so baggy that the pants would slip down when I didn't hold them up, which was hard when I was supposed to be moving rocks. We worked through the cold. I was cold all the time. My stomach hurt relentlessly. The bread I ate once a day sometimes wouldn't stay down if I ate too fast, so I hid part of it in my sleeve to take bites of throughout the rest of the day. One day I crouched down on the side of the bunkhouse hiding from the others to take a bite when the boy showed up. He watched me, still silent during the daytime hours. I ripped off a little piece and held it out to him. He snatched it quickly and stuffed it in his mouth. I offered him another piece, but he shook his head, still watching me. Then he patted my shoulder and walked away.

~~~~

Hunger, pain, exhaustion, worry. It was all I had. Another month went by and I hadn't seen my father. I knew a lot of the men were working on the other side of the camp, but the fact that I hadn't seen him riddled me with anxiety. I needed to know he was okay. To see he was okay.

Alfred and I spoke every night. He would tell me about his family, his home. I told him about mine. He kept asking me to point out my father to him so he knew who he was and I promised I would if I saw him.

One night he asked, "Do you think we could be brothers?"

"We sort of are already, aren't we?" I laid on my back, staring into the darkness.

"When we get out of here I mean. Since I won't have a mother or father. Do you think yours would take me?"

I hadn't cried for weeks, because I had grown almost numb to any type of emotion. But his simple request so full of hope broke my heart. "Of course they would."

He said nothing more, but I could feel the bunk shake from his sobs. I reached out and took his hand and was not ashamed to do so.

The one thing that the Nazis had going for them that would surely kill more Jews than anything else was the loss of hope. I saw it every day. But the other side to that was the incredible power of hope. I saw people who should have been dead, but the light was still in their eyes. The light of hope. That's the only way I can describe it. Walking corpses with the light of hope. I saw it. I know it's what kept them alive. Fathers and mothers keeping hope they would see their child again, children knowing their parents must still be alive waiting on them to come back to them. That bond of love that no man could beat out of a person was what kept the hope alive.

Several months had passed with no sign of my father. Each day of his absence added to my uncertainty of his life. There were days where my mind ran wild with the ideas of what could have happened to him. But most days, I was numb. I kept my thoughts devoid of human attachment, speaking to no one. I would pay special attention to the dirt under my nails and the way my arms ached as I used the shovel. Or the way the wind sounded or the way it carried a leaf across the field. Anything to not feel the absence of my family.

On another typical morning in the spring we were lined up waiting to count off in the yard outside the bunker when I saw him. Or a shadow of him. My father, once a strong man who carried me on his shoulders was now standing in line for his cup of morning coffee, hunched over, nothing but skin and bones. He looked like most of the men who had been here a while, the skin literally hanging off the sharp cuts of bone underneath. I searched his face making sure it was really him because he was nearly unrecognizable. I was not able to get his attention, but I saw him glancing around, perhaps looking for me. I wanted to run to him, the compulsion nearly as strong as my need to stay out of trouble, which surely I would be in if I had left the line. A lump rose in my throat.

"Go!" I hadn't noticed the line in front of me had moved until an SS guard yelled and snapped me to attention.

I rushed forward, trying to keep an eye on Papa and just as I entered the bunker he saw me. He straightened and yelled something, but I was pushed through the door and out of his sight. I kept my emotions in check, but inside, oh, my soul cried in relief that he was still alive but also it cried out in pain of the wasted state of his body.

It felt like hours before I was let back out of the bunker. I ran around, looking for him until an officer made me get back in line to march to the field for work. I kept my eyes up the whole time we worked, praying I would see him again. I didn't that day and went to bed with a heavy heart.

That night I told Alfred all about it while lying there. "I'm glad for you," he said and I knew he meant it.

Chapter Twenty-Two

Alfred was not looking well. "You feeling okay?" I asked him as we worked the next day. He dragged his feet as we walked to a new area where we were to dig ditches.

"Seriously? Does anyone here feel okay?" It was his attempt at a joke and one of the only times I saw him smile.

"Try to keep up with me. I'll do your workload, so keep close. When the officer comes around, look like you're doing something. Okay?"

He nodded and did as I had said. We began to dig, and I wondered what the purpose of these ditches were. It was hard work when you were so underfed, but for poor Alfred who was small and sick, it took a toll. He slowed, barely lifting any dirt with his shovel.

"Fill the shovel!" an officer barked. Alfred struggled, but was able to manage to do as he was commanded. The officer, apparently satisfied for the moment, strolled down the line, shouting more orders.

"Keep up, Alfred," I whispered when the guard was out of earshot.

"I don't think I can." Sweat poured down his face and he seemed unsteady.

"Just hang on. Keep going."

He nodded, but I knew there was no way he would be able to last nine more hours like that.

A few minutes later, the same guard came by and saw him struggling again. He shoved Alfred, who was down a couple feet in the ditch, with the toe of his boot and found no resistance from Alfred who went face first into the freshly upturned soil. Before I knew what was happening he took Alfred by the collar and yanked him out of the line.

His eyes grew wide with panic, looking at me over his shoulder as they pushed him along away from the group. My heart stopped, panic seizing hold of me as well. I couldn't look in his eyes anymore, so my gaze shifted to the dirt being kicked up around his feet as he struggled to free himself. But his weak, starved self was no match for the officer who all but carried him down the line where the ditch had been dug to a suitable depth.

"This is what happens if you don't work," the guard yelled out. With not even a blink of an eye, the guard turned Alfred around to face the ditch, pressed his gun to the back of his shaved head and pulled the trigger. Alfred's body crumpled into the ditch where it would remain.

That night his bunk was empty. The next day, it was filled by someone else.

~~~~

I refused to make friends again. There was no point when everyone I loved kept being ripped away from me. I added Alfred to part of The Gone and just kept to myself. I did what the officers told me like I had promised my father. But the light was beginning to dim. I could feel the hope fading and it scared me and beckoned me at the same time. The thought of being done, welcoming death, was an alluring thought. It wouldn't be long before I was dead anyway. I could barely muster enough energy to do what they wanted me to do. But then I thought of my father. What if he held on for me, enduring this torture and I gave up? What would become of him then? And what about my mother and sisters? It was a possibility, although a slim one, that they were still alive somewhere.

Another month passed of hanging on to the very thinning wire of hope. Until there came a day that death seemed the only option for me. I had been told I wouldn't go to the field that day; that I would be helping in the yard. But I was sick. Which was nothing new, it was just especially bad that day. I had to keep running to the latrine, trying to sneak away when the officers wouldn't see me. When you couldn't work, you disappeared. My body shook with fever and it was something I couldn't control. Just as I thought I could make it a little longer, my stomach cramped and I had no choice but to run to the latrine. Hurrying as fast as I could, I fell because my legs just plain couldn't keep up. I struggled, trying to pull myself up but it was no use and I messed myself right there in the dirt in front of my group. It may not have been something so out of the usual for us to see, but it was me. It was my dignity and it was gone now.

That's when I welcomed death. Beckoned it even. I didn't have long to entertain the thought before an officer came and dragged me to a truck where I was loaded into the back and taken to a bunker. "I've got another one that needs washing," said the man who transported me there as he shoved me towards another guard before turning around and leaving.

The building was one I had seen before, but never been in. It was the same bunker that thick twists of smoke rose from along with a horrendous smell. I stood in the back of a line with a few people, an officer in the front, one in the back next to me. I wasn't sure what was taking so long, but we stood there waiting for the door to open. Trucks were parked around the building which was farther away from the rest of the camp. I looked around, feeling uneasy, that something was off. My stomach cramped again and I doubled over in pain until I fell to my knees.

"Stand!" But I couldn't.

"Leo, stand up!" My father's voice. He was behind me, lifting me up somehow even though he looked as though he'd break from the movement.

"Don't take him. I'll help him." My father pleaded to the officer.

"Nein. He goes."

"Then I go too." My father straightened up as best he could, lifting his chin.

The officer gave him a once over and nodded. Then my father took my hand for the first time in months and repeated the words he said when we first were taken. "Don't let go of my hand no matter what." I clung on with a fierceness that only love can produce because I was scared. So scared it was sucking the life out of me. In that moment I realized that was it. It was the end. Why else would my father dare to stand up to the officer just over a shower? I'd heard the rumors. The dread of the unknown sank in and settled in my bones. I had always known what the building was used for, but had lied to myself so many times, not wanting to believe the place really existed. I lied to myself every day to the point I had started believing it myself. This day however, the sick reality hit me like a ton of bricks and I realize my wishing for death had come to fruition.

Suddenly the door swung open. "Go!" The men ushered us inside another room. Once inside, the door slammed shut, making me jump. "Take off your clothes." We looked around at each other, perhaps looking to see if anyone dared refute the orders.

"Now!" The command was all we needed to comply.

I slipped off my soiled pants and kicked them to the side, hoping no one would notice. It's silly now to think that is what I was worried about in that moment. Thoughts of myself quickly turned to my father when I saw his emaciated body. He had wasted away. Skin hung in loose folds around his stomach and from his hips. Where muscles had once been in his arms, now only bone and skin remained. It was something from a nightmare and I couldn't stand to look at him. Anger bubbled up in my chest, expanding, threatening to blow up and destroy everything in its sight. My father must have thought the same when he saw me because he said, "Where is God?"

The people around me were children and sick adults. Some who were barely standing. We shook, our bodies cold and scared. Eyes with no lights on. Hope was something that didn't exist in that room. Not for us shivering, cold and naked. Nowhere to run. It was time to accept what was to happen.

The door on the opposite side of the room opened and I saw shower heads running the length of the wall. Relief flooded over me, hoping maybe that was all we were there for, to shower. But then my father said again, "Just hold on. Don't let go of my hand." He was nervous. So nervous I could feel it. It scared me, knowing something bad must be coming.

I looked at the tattoo on his arm, in the same place as mine, as we held hands and I closed my eyes, waiting for whatever came next. I heard the door slam shut behind us and I jumped again, but kept my eyes closed. Overhead I heard something on the ceiling, but still no water from the showers. A man began to wail and panic was invited in. There was a terrible commotion and I couldn't help but open my eyes to see what was going on.

An officer stood in a doorway on the opposite side of where we came in and was motioning for us to get out. "Go. Hurry. Go." There were only eight of us and it took us a minute to move, but realizing the urgency in his voice we did as we were told. My father let out a sort of whimper, as if he was going to cry and pushed me in front of him.

"Go, Leo. Hurry."

I didn't hesitate, but as we entered the next room, I wanted to turn back. Bodies, dozens of bodies piled on the floor and the thick smell of smoke assaulted my nose. I must have slowed because my father pushed me and said, "Don't look. Keep going. Hurry!"

I ran, catching up to the others in front of us. The officer ushered us outside and into the back of a truck that was waiting right outside the door. We piled in without question, perhaps knowing anywhere was better than were we had just been.

"I'm sorry, but I must do this," the guard said as he was joined by a couple of prisoners, Sonderkommandos, who began piling a dozen corpses on top of us. "Stay still and don't say a thing," he instructed when they had finished.

"What's going on, Papa?" I whispered. "I'm scared."

"Shhh."

The truck shifted into gear and we rolled forward. I felt like I was suffocating under the weight of the corpses. The smell so nauseating, the bodies, though they were mostly bones really, pressed down on me to where I felt as though I might lose my mind. I had a brief moment where I thought of knocking everything off of me just to get a breath of fresh air, but my terror of being caught stopped me.

A few moments passed before the truck stopped. I heard the driver say, "Crematorium is backed up. I'll drop these in the field on my way home."

A few pleasantries and a bid good afternoon were said before the truck rumbled through the gates. We went a bit longer before the truck stopped abruptly.

"Remain quiet," he whispered. "You two, come!" He yelled to someone else.

The load was lightened one body at a time before we saw the sky and it was the most beautiful sky I'd ever seen. Azure broken up by white puffy clouds. The two prisoners didn't blink an eye when they uncovered us. For some reason, it wasn't until that moment that I realized it was all planned out. All those prisoners and the guard in on the escape. Even when I thought it, I didn't quite believe it.

We weren't there in the field but three, four minutes tops before we drove off again. This time covered by a tarp. Still naked, cold and shivering from fever, but alive.

We eight remained quiet for at least thirty minutes before I broke the silence. "What is happening?"

"I think God finally heard my prayers." Then my father sobbed against my chest.

Chapter Twenty-Three

The truck ride took over an hour or so. We were hot and the smell was abysmal, making me gag and dry heave several times. I was so weak from being sick and not having eaten in such a long time that I really thought death was coming for me in the back of that truck. It wasn't that I wasn't getting my daily rations, it was that they went straight through me.

When the vehicle finally stopped and the engine cut off, there was a moment of uncertainty. I believe we all thought we were being taken away from the camp, but to what fate? What interest did this officer have in smuggling us out?

The tarp lifted and we were met by the officer's face and another man. "Out quickly!" The problem was we were all sick and weak and were incapable of moving quickly. I scampered down and the two men helped my father out of the truck and it was then I saw we were at a home in the thick of the woods with no other houses in sight.

"Inside!" The men directed us in through the front door and up the stairs.

Once we were gathered in a bedroom, the man, whose house I assumed it was, said, "Welcome home, brothers."

The officer nodded, then turned and left. It was the last time I saw him, but I will never forget his face. We were allowed to bathe, given clean, new clothes, none of which fit us well. But we didn't care. They didn't have stripes or stars. Then we were given broth and bread and it was as though manna from heaven rained upon us. My father wept. He looked as though he should be dead, dark circles under his sunken eyes, tears rolling down his sharp, protruding cheekbones. I couldn't stop staring at him, wondering if I was as frightening to look at as he was to me.

That night we slept in a hidden room upstairs on the floor, but on mattresses. It seemed like it had been forever since I slept on a comfortable surface.

"Papa? What do we do now? Can we go home?"

"No, Leo. We can't go home. Not yet."

"Where do you think Mama and Ania and Cyryl are?"

He was silent for a long moment before saying, "Hopefully somewhere much better than we were."

I slept that night in the arms of my father and I, a fifteen-year-old boy, had never felt anything better.

~~~~

A few days passed and my father wasn't feeling well. Well, he was feeling worse. My stomach still wasn't right, but I felt some sort of strength coming back. The man who had taken us in was a Christian. The officer who had brought us here was a Nazi. And we soon learned this was not the first time they had done this.

"Why would they risk their life, Papa? Won't they be punished if they are caught?"

He nodded. "Yes. They'll kill them. But sometimes people do the right thing because they are good human beings. And sometimes they realize the punishment by man is nothing compared to the punishment of God."

"Why were you there? How did we end up at the same place?" It seemed impossible to me that we should end up in the same place where we would be whisked away to safety.

"I was working there. I have been in the gas chambers for the past three months and knew my time was about to expire. Once chosen as a Sonderkommando your time is limited to four months since you have a look into the running of the camp. They don't want us to know too much. Afraid we'll use that knowledge to fight back. One day I had witnessed the goodness of the guard. I heard he was working with many in the resistance. So I approached him, knowing I had nothing to lose at that point. I begged him to find you and get you here the next time he planned an escape. I knew it was a risk, but like I said, I had nothing to lose. They would kill me soon enough."

He must have noticed how this disturbed me because he reached over and tousled my hair. "We made it. Unless this is the best dream of my life, we did it."

~~~~

Papa gave me his supper that night. "You eat. I'm too sick to keep it down and you need it. You're a growing boy."

I tried to protest, but did as he said.

The next day he didn't get out of bed.

"What's wrong?" I asked, but he just shook his head.

The owner brought up some broth around noon and sat next to Papa's mattress. "Try this."

Papa refused. "I can't. I'm not hungry anyway. Give it to someone else."

I wiped at his brow, slick with sweat, with a cloth. "Papa, please, you need to eat. You have to get better."

He reached out and rested his hand on the side of my face. "Listen, my son. The only reason I didn't die the first month in that Hell was because of you. You were my reason for living. I couldn't die knowing you were living in that place. You were all I was living for. Now that you are safe, I can die in peace."

"Papa, don't talk like that. You still have Mama and Ania and Cyryl. They'll be waiting for us."

"I hope you're right, Leo. But I think you are old enough and have been through enough to realize that might not be the case."

I took his hand in mine and didn't let go while I sat with him through the next two days. I watched the life slipping away one breath at a time. In a moment of awareness he asked for the owner to come to him.

"Tell me your name and the name of the officer. When I see God, I want to personally thank Him for you both. You saved my son's life."

The man looked uncomfortable and then realized the dying man would tell no one. "My name is Karol and the officer's name is Heinz Amsel."

"Will you please look after my boy and make sure when this whole thing is over, he is well and taken care of?"

"Of course."

That night, his breath would stop for seconds at a time then start back up again. The throaty rattle told me what I feared the most. I knew what the sound meant. Laying my head against his chest, I grabbed his hand and squeezing tight said, "Whatever you do, don't let go of my hand. I won't let go, Papa."

Chapter Twenty-Four

I spent the next eleven months in the home, where I gained weight, met several new people that came. Some were like my father who were just too close to the brink of death to bring them back. We helped make wooden chairs for Karol to sell to assist with the costs of housing and feeding us and it became therapeutic to me.

Sanding, shaving, cutting the wood, shaping it however I wanted, created an outlet where all I could think about was how I was to work the wood. I tried valiantly to not let my thoughts wander. Many times I thought of joining my father, and for all I knew, the rest of my family as well. But to think of my father's will to go through Hell and back to make sure I made it out of the camp snuffed those self-pitying notions of ending my life. It was no longer an option.

Things I did think about as I worked with the wood was my future and what I would do about it. The thought of the war ending and me being able to go about free again was a struggle. It was rumored, but the glimmer of hope scared me; afraid I wouldn't see it, that we would be found out, or that it just wouldn't happen at all. Perhaps I would spend the rest of my life in the forest making furniture.

~~~~

When the war ended and the concentration camps were freed, I stood in the empty room, the last one of the refugees to leave. Karol held out his hand and shook mine. "Go, Leo. Have a good life." I was only seventeen, but a man by any rights.

"Thank you, Karol. May you be blessed for what you have done."

He hugged me with wet eyes and sent me off with a bag of food and a little money.

The road was long. It took me a good week to make it back to my hometown. As I approached my city, I saw the devastating toll the war had taken on it. Once beautiful buildings, now just piles of rubble and ash. If it hadn't been for the sign still marking my town, I would have thought I was in the wrong place, a world away.

I walked down my street, heartbroken at the sight of it all. When I reached our home, I half expected my mother and sisters to be there waiting at the window for me. But all I found was the burned down pile of stone that looked just like the rest of the town. I saw a woman, thin and dirty sitting down the road and ran to her.

It was my best friend's mother. As I approached, she looked up, tears running down her face. "Leo?"

I nodded.

"They're all gone," she said. "All of them."

I reached out to hug her and she clung to me, grabbing fistfuls of my shirt in her fists. "They are all gone!"

We sat that way for a while in the wreckage of our town, homes, our families. The wind blew through the piles of dust and rustled the scarf on her head. The loneliness was palpable. It took me awhile before I mustered up the courage to ask. "Do you know what became of my mother and sisters?" I'd guessed they had been taken to the same place she had.

Her brown eyes filled with tears when she looked at me. Reaching out to me, she patted my cheek and said, "They're gone as well."

Hope. Where was it? It seeped from me like water in a cracked bucket. Should I even fight to keep the last shred of it I had? Did it even matter anymore?

We parted ways. I could have stayed with her. But what was the point? We couldn't fill the void of The Gone and we would just end up being reminders of the mother and son we had lost. I think she understood that as well. There was one more reminder I needed to get rid of.

That night I lit a fire amongst the rubble, took a piece of metal and bathed it in the flames. When it was nice and hot, I pressed it against the black prisoner number on my arm. A scar was better than the tattoo. I would no longer be just a number to the regime.

I walked for days, hungry, rationing my meager stash of money until I ended up back at the house in the woods. When he opened the door, he sighed and welcomed me into his home for the second time.

I stayed with him for nearly three more years, making and selling furniture. We made very little money, but what I did make I saved. I knew exactly what I wanted to do with the stash, but I had to be patient.

~~~~

The year I turned twenty-one years old I decided it was time for me to leave the house in the woods. Before going I asked Karol, "Where can I find the officer? Heinz Amsel?"

He leaned back into his chair and looked at me for a moment, eyes narrowed. "What is this about?"

"I want to thank him for what he did. For saving my father and I. If it weren't for him, I never would have been able to spend a few days with my father before he died. I would have never seen him again."

"I'm not sure where he is. He disappeared shortly after you arrived. Remember, he only brought two more truckloads of people after you? But I believe he's from the town of Lobau, Germany. At least he mentioned it once before. That's all I know of him. Maybe he has family there."

That night I decided to go find the man and thank him. I felt it like a pull towards my purpose. That God was speaking to me, telling me to move on and stop hiding in the forest. I knew I needed to figure out what I was to do with my life, but I had no idea. The only thing that kept coming back to mind was the officer's name. So I followed the pull.

"You come back any time. I can always use the help with the furniture." Karol sent me off with a hug and kiss on the cheek.

Chapter Twenty-Five

I made my way to Germany with what little I had. I had no papers, so I became whoever was most convenient at the time. I worked odd jobs and tried to keep under the radar while I roamed. I traded work for a meal or a place to stay. Sometimes staying in barns for months at a time when I had a good place of employment.

In the year of 1951 I met a man who needed help in his bakery for several weeks while his wife recovered from an illness. I took the job, him showing me what to do and me trying to do it correctly. Horst was a tall man with arms the size of tree trunks. His grip was firm, his arms and head covered in dark, thick hair. It was a strange sight seeing his giant hands work the dough over and put little icing roses on a cake. He was skilled though, so I tried to pay attention and do my best to learn the workings of the shop.

The first day I worked alone in the bakery, the bell above the door rang and I looked up to find a beautiful nineteen-year-old girl come in. I was punching down the bread, which I was late getting in the oven because I had ruined the first batch. The girl had black curly hair around a face that was as pretty as any I had ever seen.

Eyes like a brown-eyed doe and cheeks blushed. A few freckles were scattered across her nose and the apples of her cheeks as if they were applied as an artist's afterthought. Not quite expected, but beautifying anyway. "Hello."

It took me a minute to realize she spoke to me even though we were the only ones in the shop. "Good morning."

"You must be the new man Horst hired?"

"That I am. What can I get for you?"

She eyed the near empty case of breads. "Not too much to choose from today." Her dark brown eyes danced when she smiled as she held out her hand. "I'm Elke."

I brushed the flour from my hands before taking hers. "Leo. Nice to meet you, Miss Elke."

"Have you ever worked in a bakery before?" Her smile never faltered, but now it turned more into a teasing tug at her lips.

"Never."

"Hmm. I wonder if I should come back later."

"The owner will be here soon to help if you would like to wait." I smiled back at her hoping she would accept my invitation.

"No he won't. But how about if I help you? You look like you could use it."

She walked around the counter and put her purse in the office, returning with an apron on.

"I really could use the help, but I don't know if it's a good idea for you to be back here."

She reached around me, grabbing a bowl off the shelf and as she did, I caught the slightest scent of her perfume and I was done. I hadn't been so close to a girl since I was a boy. And somehow time had changed the way I felt about it and the way my body reacted to it.

"I'm Horst's daughter. He asked me to come in today because he has some things to do." She threw a smile at me before sinking her fists into the mound of dough. I watched her work. She was so efficient and graceful in her movements around the kitchen. There was no frenzied rush to get things done, which was how I felt before she got there. I couldn't take my eyes off her as she tossed flour over the dough, kneaded it, flipped it over, floured more, and kneaded again. The movements were all fluid and I could tell she had grown up there, in the bakery.

While we worked, we spoke about her family and what goes on in the small village, but then settled into a quiet rhythm, occasionally bumping into each other. I felt like an ox. She was so at ease that I should have been too, but the feelings stirring up inside of me were anything but calm.

We worked with each other for three more days before her father returned to work. On that first day without her, I found myself thinking of nothing else and wondering how I could possibly get to see her more. She made it a little easier because she would stop by the shop often. Her father giving us both the eye when we spoke or smiled at one another.

That night after I had put my jacket on and settled my hat down he called me back into his office. "Leo, can I have a word with you?"

"Yes Sir."

"You will stay away from my daughter." His dark eyes narrowed in on me and I knew this was a man I didn't want to cross.

"Yes Sir."

He stared me down for another minute before waving me off.

As I stepped out of the shop, Elke was waiting for me. I stopped, not quite knowing what I should do.

"Hello, Leo."

I tipped my hat. "Hello."

Her eyes dropped to the toe of her shoe with which she was drawing a circle on the sidewalk. "I was just on my way home and was wondering if you would like to walk me."

I glanced over my shoulder, worrying that her father would see us. When I looked back, she looked at me with eyes that I couldn't refuse.

I smiled and started walking. Her home was only down the street, but any amount of time I could get with her was good for me. I glanced back three times in a span of two minutes. "Sure is a nice night," I said when we got to her door.

"Will you take me somewhere sometime?" Her smile was back. It was such a brazen question for her to be asking me and I felt like we were doing this all backwards. Even though I had never dated a girl, I still felt like it wasn't quite right.

"I don't think that's a great idea. Your father told me to stay away from you. I shouldn't even have walked you home." I glanced back towards the shop, half expecting her father to be running towards us ready to lay me out right there on the sidewalk.

I didn't even have a chance to look back before I felt her take my hand and drag me around to the side of the house.

Hidden mostly in the dark of the night she faced me and said, "Have you ever had a girlfriend, Leo?"

I shook my head.

"Do you want one?" She took a step towards me and my nerves started buzzing with the inches between us.

"Let me worry about my father. He'll come around. In the meantime we can meet here every night after work. He stays for at least another hour so that will give us plenty of time to see each other." She stepped even closer.

I nodded. Not thinking a single thought about her father, only her beautiful face and how she smelled and the curve of her lips.

She smiled a smile that could light up the world and then reached up on her tip toes, pressing her lips against mine. It only lasted a few seconds, but it was enough to hook me. She ran back to her house as I stood there with a stupid grin on my face. It was my first kiss, but most definitely not my last with Elke.

Chapter Twenty-Six

It went on like that for weeks. Sneaking glances, kisses, moments. It was intoxicating. It was all I thought about day and night. Her mother was getting better and I knew it wouldn't be long before I would be out of a job again and wondered where I would go from there.

One night we met in secret at the theater and sat in the back, kissing and talking, paying no attention to the film.

"Will you stay when my mother comes back to the bakery?"

"I don't see how I can."

She became quiet and then I realized what an idiot I had been.

"What's wrong?"

She wouldn't meet my eyes. "You're leaving me?"

"I have to. I'll need to find another job and…"

She dropped my hand and turned rigid in her seat, facing the screen. I watched her for a moment as the light flickered across her face. "I'm sorry. I didn't mean to hurt you."

"Why don't you take me with you?"

I had been so caught up in this fun, new discovery of feelings for the opposite sex I hadn't taken time to think about what it meant for her. "Your father would never allow it."

She looked hard at me then grabbed her handbag and stormed out of the theater.

I caught up to her on the street. "Elke. Stop. Please just talk to me."

"I should have listened to my father. He told me you were no good and would only leave. I'm such a foolish girl." She quickened her pace until I grasped her elbow and stopped her.

"Please look at me." I waited until she did. "You are a terrific girl who has given me so much. You will always hold a special place in my heart. But I can't give you what you want. You want to get married and I am a man with no home and no money. No way to provide for you or a family. I'm still trying to get my own stuff together. We really don't even know each other." It was true. She didn't even know I was Jewish. I kept my scarred-over tattoo covered. I had dodged all questions about the war and my family. She assumed they still lived back in Poland and I let her believe it. It was a whole lot less complicated that way.

"Then why did you even do this? Why make me believe I was something special when you were just planning on leaving the whole time?"

I took her by the shoulders. "You *are* special. I had never even thought of a girl the way I think about you. Never even kissed a girl."

Her eyes narrowed. "If that's all I was for you, then I'm glad you're leaving."

I raked my hands through my hair and sighed. "That's not what I meant. I have feelings for you, but I think we both know this isn't going to work out. I am just not in a position to provide for you. You are a terrific girl and you deserve someone so much better than me." I went to touch her shoulder again, but she shrugged me off.

"Don't. Don't tell me how great I am because in the end I'm still not great enough to make you stay. So let's just chalk this up to what it is and say goodbye." Her eyes were cold and I died a little inside seeing how hurt she was. Especially because it was my fault.

"I'm so sorry."

"So am I." She walked away and I let her go. Everything in me wanted to go after her, but I knew it would only make it worse, because in the end, it was not meant to be. That was the last time I would see Elke. She stayed away from the bakery for the next week and a half until Horst let me go.

So I set out to Germany again with a little more money in my pocket and the memories of what it felt like to kiss a woman.

Chapter Twenty-Seven

I found the town I wanted. It was a small town in Germany that fared much better than mine. I stopped at the post office and found a woman at the front desk. I was nervous, wondering if she knew I was a Jew; wondered if the fact that I had escaped the camp was written across my forehead. Even though the war had ended long before, it was a feeling I couldn't shake; being on the run.

"Excuse me, I was wondering if you could tell me where I might find someone by the name of Amsel?"

She barely glanced at me before scrawling something on a piece of paper and handing it to me. "That way." She pointed west and turned back to her stack of letters she was sorting.

I nodded, relieved to get out of there without incident.

There weren't many people out, being that it was an early spring day and there was a bite in the air. But just as I rounded the corner of the street I was looking for, I saw two men in uniform knock on the door of the home of my destination. I hung back a little, not wanting trouble. It was risky coming here and I had second thoughts. I was a free man, but as soon as I saw the bands on the arms of the uniformed men, I was a prisoner back in Hell. I decided to come back later and turned around. Just as I reached the corner heading back, I heard the scream of a woman come from inside the house. I quickened my pace, back in the direction of the commotion and eased up to the side of the house. Making my way around to the back, I stopped when I saw through the kitchen window, an older woman tied up and the two men ransacking her home.

The men flipped over the table, spilling her cup of tea, the cup shattering. "Tell us where he is!"

"I do not know," she pleaded. "I speak the truth."

One of the men got closer, right in her face. "You lie," he spit.

Then the other man, the shorter one disappeared for a few minutes before returning with several letters in his hand. "Who do you write to in America?"

"Family. But not who you are looking for. When he left, I never saw or heard from him again."

The taller man stepped up and slapped her face with the back of his hand. "If we find out you lied, we will kill you." With a kick to a kitchen chair in his way, they left with the stack of letters in hand.

I stayed out of view as they walked down the street and when I felt it was safe to go in, I entered from the back kitchen door. She froze when she saw me and said, "I promise. I don't know where he is."

I put my finger to my lips. "I'll help you. I'm not here to hurt you."

After untying her, I peeked out the window again; making sure the men weren't coming back. To my relief, they were still walking in the opposite direction.

"Who are you?" she asked.

"I was actually looking for a man with the last name of Amsel."

"I told you, I haven't heard from him since he disappeared."

I held up my hands, worried she would get louder and alert the men. "Like I said, I'm not here to hurt you. I was looking for him to thank him. He helped me a few years ago and I just wanted to thank him and shake his hand. That's all."

She studied me for a minute before saying, "I still can't help you. But I'm sure he would be happy to know he helped you." She didn't ask questions about how he helped me, but I got the feeling she knew exactly what I spoke about.

I knew she wasn't going to tell me where he was even if she did know.

As I left her house, I kept an eye out for the men, making sure they didn't see me leaving. They weren't on the street at all, but as I got into town I saw them enter a beer hall and decided to follow.

Inside, the air was stale and heavy, dark, but I saw the two men bellied up to the bar and I shoved down any fear and doubt and did the same, sitting a few stools away.

After ordering a round of beer, they spread the letters in front of them. The shorter one said, "It's got to be him."

The taller one, "I'm not sure. But I guess it wouldn't hurt to check it out. I will go to America and find him and when I do, I will slit his throat for my father."

They clinked glasses together, tossed back their heads and drank.

~~~~

I followed the tall one for a week. Sleeping outside his house, staying low. I'm not sure what I expected to get from it, but I had nothing as it was. I wanted to find out what happened to Officer Amsel and it seemed as though the tall man would lead me right to him.

Then one day, he went back to the woman's house. I snuck around to the back again and listened. He slapped a couple pieces of paper in front of her. "Copy this word for word and sign your name."

"What are you going to—" She wasn't able to finish before he struck her face.

"Do it. Now."

She trembled as she took the pen in her hand and I wished I could see what she was writing.

When she finished the man picked it up and looked it over. Apparently satisfied, he took his gun out from the back of his pants, pressed a pillow against her forehead, then the muzzle of the gun and pulled the trigger. Feathers spread across the room and floated down to the floor, where the elderly woman lay.

The man took the papers, shoved his gun back where it had been, dusted off the feathers from his clothes and shoes and walked out the door. I knew there was no helping the woman just by looking at her. I added her to my list of The Gone and grieved for her. Then I picked myself up from the crouched position below the window, bottled my seething anger and followed the man again.

~~~~

Two weeks later he boarded a ship bound for America and I did the same. I followed him, watched how he interacted, studied him. And the second night when he joined a few men for drinks, I did also.

"This next round is on me if I can get in on the next game of poker."

I slapped his back as I sat next to him. He leaned back, taken by surprise and then raised his glass to me. "You're in." And there I sat with a few former Nazi soldiers and me, a Jew, pretending not to be. I hid my accent well, adapting to their German easily. It was drilled into me every second I was in the camp after all. We got talking about the war and I told them how my Nazi father had been assigned to Auschwitz and how he was my hero.

"Maybe he knew my father. That's where he was stationed for a while."

"Good man, I bet he was. What's your name?"

"Max. Yours?"

"Klein. Good to know you."

Then we smoked our cigars like old friends all the while I fantasized about all the ways I could kill him.

As we talked I wondered who his father was. If he was at the same camp I was then I had probably seen him at some point. Was he the one who kicked Alfred when he dropped his bread and was on all fours trying to salvage it from the dirt? The one who sent me to the gas chamber? Though, I suppose in a way I should thank that one. It is what led to my finding my father and escaping. I dissected Max's features, trying to match them with the Nazis in camp and something did seem familiar, but I just couldn't place it.

"So what's taking you to America?" I asked him.

"Getting married."

Didn't expect that. "You don't say?"

"Yes, sir. Got a girl and a nice piece of a land waiting for me."

I whistled. "You are a lucky man."

He downed another shot of vodka and wiped at his mouth with the back of his hand before slamming the glass down. "Not luck, my man, it's all about making it happen for yourself. What about you?"

"I have family I'm visiting. I'm still haven't decided if I'll stay in America or not."

Our conversation was cut off when a man bumped into the back of me, spilling his drink in my lap.

"I'm going to go change. Will you be around for a game of poker in a bit?"

Max looked at me and raised his glass. "Of course, brother."

The word made me want to spit in his face, but I refrained. There would be a time. It just wasn't yet.

Chapter Twenty-Eight

We met each night for a game of poker where the men did nothing but get drunk and lose their money. I played the part, but stayed sober. I still wanted to know how he knew Amsel and find out what he wanted from him.

One night while helping him back to his cabin because he was so smashed, I asked him since we were alone and I didn't have to worry about the other men becoming suspicious. "This girl, your fiancé, how did you meet?"

"We haven't." He put his finger to his lips and laughed. "She thinks I'm coming to marry her because her parents died. Really I'm just tying up some loose ends of my fathers'. We had an unsettled debt with her father. I wanted to show up to off him, but the lucky SOB went and got himself killed in a car accident before I could get my hands on him."

I dropped him on his bed harder than I intended to, but he was too drunk to realize. "What did he do?"

"Because of him, my father was executed for crossing the regime. The pig lied to my father who helped cover for him by telling him he was coming back. But he never did and my father was held accountable for it. He was a Jew lover and lied to my father. And because of that, they shot him between the eyes." He closed his own eyes, throwing his arm across them. "Turn off the light on your way out."

The no good, sloppy drunk of a Nazi. I should have killed him then. But I didn't. Instead I waited until his guard was down even more.

~~~~

The next night followed just like the ones before. Poker game, beer, vodka, drunk imbeciles. Once again, I volunteered to assist Max to his cabin. "Wait. I want to stay here just one more moment." He plucked his cigar from his front pocket and tried to light it, but couldn't steady his hand long enough before the match burned out.

I took the matches from his hands and said, "Here, let me help."

"I'll be glad when I'm off this damn boat."

"Yes. I know what you mean."

"She better not be ugly," he muttered.

He took a puff when the cigar lit and I shook out the match. "Who?"

"The girl. The daughter I'm going to. I mean, I plan on killing her anyway, but not before I get my piece of land and take everything from that SOB Jew lover. Including her. That's why I hope she's not ugly. I might as well enjoy myself while I wait for things to get put into my name." He was quiet for a moment before saying, "I guess I could just put a bag over her head while I have my way with her." He slapped my back and laughed.

I couldn't help myself. I said it before I could think. "You're a pig."

"Excuse me?" His smile faded.

"You heard me. You're a pig." I couldn't help it any longer. I called him a pig again and spit in his face. I did it on behalf of the fifteen-year-old me not capable of spitting in the faces of the SS officers.

He grabbed my shirt and swung, but his drunkenness slowed him and I was able to get in a punch. As soon as it connected with his gut I knew there was no holding me back. The feeling so satisfying. I swung again. And again. He grappled at my shirt but it was no use. He was so wasted I could have just tipped him over with one finger. He swung again and I ducked before punching his face. The force made him stumble and before I could do anything, he lost his footing and went over the rail, plunging into the sea. I searched for him in the darkness, but couldn't see anything. The engines so loud no screams were heard. I looked around, but no one was there. There was a moment I thought about telling someone, having them stop the boat to look for him. But I didn't.

I did nothing.

~~~~

It took me just a few minutes to make a plan. I rushed to his room, went through his things and stole his ID papers along with the money and a few letters he had, which had the address of the girl. We would be arriving tomorrow by noon and I needed to be ready.

I couldn't sleep that night. I had killed a man. Yes, it wasn't intentional, and it really was an accident, but it was because we were fighting that he fell. Because I called him a pig. Which was being kind. I couldn't let myself feel bad about it, it started to cloud my judgment and I needed to have it together if I was to get off that ship.

The next day I lined up with my luggage along with the other passengers as we pulled into the harbor and one of the guys we had played poker with the previous night stood next to me. "Have you seen Max today?" He scanned the crowd looking for him.

"I haven't. He drank a lot last night though, so maybe he's moving slow today." I laughed, trying to ease the tension I felt and it must have worked because he laughed as well. I kept talking to him, trying to keep his mind off of Max, hoping he wouldn't try to go look for him. I needed to be long gone before anyone noticed him missing.

We disembarked and went through customs which was the scariest part. I had my own papers, which I had paid an unsavory soul for, before getting to Germany. I had Max's as well, tucked in the lining of my suitcase.

As soon as I was able to leave, I headed towards the train station and didn't look back.

GITA
1952

Chapter Twenty-Nine

The man standing in front of me looks uncomfortable. Sweat beads on his forehead and I realize he's probably wondering why I haven't let him in.

I can't seem to process what he's said. I stay where I am, a closed screen door between us. "Who are you again?"

"I'm Max. Your Aunt Frieda wrote to you, letting you know I would be coming. I assume the letter reached you?"

I nod. "If you are who you say you are, why weren't you here months ago like you were supposed to be?"

He shifts his weight to his other leg and says, "You mind letting me in and I'll tell you."

When I don't move he adds, "I could use a drink." He gestures around him as if he's trying to draw my attention to the hot day.

My heart pounds in protest, but I open the door anyway. "Please sit and I'll get you something to drink," I say as I start towards the kitchen.

"Thank you." His German-thick English reminds me of my parents, which also reminds me when the Max I've been living with showed up with a Polish accent instead of the German one I expected. Dread fills my chest as I realize I don't know who is telling me the truth. If the man sitting in my living room is the Max my aunt sent, then who is the man I'm married to?

I feel lightheaded. The room seems to be closing in on me and suddenly the desire to run snatches me up. I glance at the back door, but remember Max or whoever he is, took the car this morning. I have no way to run if I wanted. My hands shake as I drop a few ice cubes into a glass. Do I try to find out more from the man? Should I be afraid of him? Or more importantly, should I be afraid of the man I'm married to?

I take a deep breath before picking up the glass from the counter, ready to face the man in my house when a hand covers my mouth and another one grabs the glass from me before it drops to the floor. Panic floods my senses and I struggle against the strong arms around me.

"Shhhh. Please. Be quiet. Don't scream. I'll let go if you promise not to scream, but we must be quiet." I nod at my husband's request, even though I'm not sure what I should do, who I should flee from.

He drops his hold on me and turns me around to face him. He takes my hand and pulls me into the pantry. His dark eyes dart from me to the kitchen door as he whispers. "You have to listen. We need to leave. I'm not sure what he's told you, but I'm sure you have questions and I promise I'll answer them all. But we have to get out of here. Now."

I shake my head, not quite sure what to do. "Who are you?"

"I'm your husband. Your husband who you know and trust. Please, just come with me and I'll explain everything."

"Just tell me one thing. Are you the real Max who my aunt sent over here?"

His eyes are full of regret, fear. He's frightened and I think I already knew the answer. "No."

I back away, "How could you? I trusted you."

He grabs my arm, "Please, Gita, you have to trust me. He's here to hurt you. Please, just come with me." He places my closed fist in his and holds it against his chest. "You know *me*. Trust me."

The thoughts in my head spin around until I feel sick. I know what I need to do. I yank my hand away from his and pick up the glass of water on my way to the living room.

~~~~

I paint a smile on my face when I round the corner, trying to hide the frantic nerves coursing through my body. "You'll have to excuse me. I wasn't expecting you."

"Like I said, there was an incident that kept me from coming here or sending word for that matter. I had lost your address and it took some time to find you." He takes a long pull of water and I watch as he taps his finger against the glass. The beads of sweat keep coming and he wipes them away with the back of his forearm.

I sit across the room from him in the armchair. I have a view of both him and the kitchen and I wonder what the Max I know will do. Is he waiting in the kitchen or has he left?

"So please, do tell me what happened. What is this incident you speak of?" My heart pounds as I listen and watch his body language, which is becoming more uncomfortable by the minute.

He shifts in his seat before saying, "I was thrown from the ship. Someone tried to kill me by throwing me overboard and leaving me to drown. I, however, was fortunate enough to have come across a piece of driftwood. I was able to stay afloat until a ship spotted me the next day. I had been floating atop the piece of wood unconscious and dehydrated and beat up. The man who did it has yet to be caught." He takes another drink, finishing it off. I don't miss the resentment in his eyes.

I stand and reach out for his empty cup. "Let me get you another. Are you hungry?"

A slow smile spreads his lips and instantly the hairs on the back of my neck prickle. "I could use something to eat. Mind if I wash up?"

I point him in the direction of the bathroom and rush into the kitchen. I find Max, my husband, standing near the back door. I don't hesitate as I rush over to him, pushing him out the door. "Leave."

"No. I'm not leaving you with that—"

I rush to explain. "I need to get him out of here so that we can leave. But only if you answer one question for me first."

He nods, hope lighting his eyes.

"Can I trust you?"

"One hundred percent." He looks at me with such intensity and I know I can.

"Stay out of sight. I will get rid of him and then we will figure out what to do."

"I'll be right here. If you need anything, just yell."

"I'll be fine." Before stepping through the door I turn to him. "You better not make me regret this."

~~~~

The new Max strides down the hall and stands in the doorway to the kitchen.

"I'm sorry, but I need to go into town for some food. It seems I'm out of everything. Are you staying at the hotel in town?"

"I am."

"Good. Perhaps we can meet there for dinner tonight. I will get ready and meet you there."

"I can wait."

I smile. "Thank you, but if you don't mind I'm a little uncomfortable with you staying here when we barely know each other. Let's meet at the hotel tonight at seven and we'll make arrangements from there."

I can see the hesitation, the internal conflict by the way he looks at me, eyes narrowed, scrutinizing me. "Very well. I look forward to tonight." He reaches for my hand and I allow him to take it and bring it to his lips.

Every part of my body is telling me not to trust him. There's nothing about him that puts my body at ease.

"Until tonight then," I say as I walk him to the door.

I watch as he gets into his car and drives away before rushing to the back door. Max, the one I know, is already in the kitchen.

"Thank you for believing me. I know you didn't have to and I—"

I raise my hand to stop him. "You better start explaining and if I don't like what I hear, you promise you will leave."

"I promise."

"Then talk."

"I will. I will tell you everything, but I think we need to leave. I'll explain it in the car. The man is dangerous and I don't want to take a chance that he'll come back. We need some distance while I explain everything and make a plan."

I study his face, his pleading eyes, the ones I've trusted for the past few months. "Do I need to pack a bag?"

"Take anything you wouldn't want to live without because I'm not sure how long we'll be gone." When I don't move he says, "I promise, you can trust me."

Before Max runs to get the car, he explains to me that when he saw the unknown car in front of the house on his way home from town, he turned off our dirt road and hid the car in the grove of trees. While he's gone I grab some clothes, pictures, mother's ring, the tin of money from under the floorboard and the steel black box with a lock on it, and stuff them into a suitcase.

Max returns and does the same before we hustle out to the car and toss our belongings into the trunk. I drive, even though he's become a better driver in the past few months, he still doesn't know the roads and towns like I do.

"Where should we go?" I ask, glancing in the rearview. Even though it's highly unlikely anyone is following as there are no other cars in sight. I still can't shake the feeling someone is following us.

"Anywhere. At least a couple hours away."

I notice he's checking the mirrors as well.

"There's a hotel in Frost where my parents and I once stayed. It's out of the way, not too many people would come across it."

"That sounds perfect."

"You have until we reach the hotel, which if I remember correctly is a little over three hours away, to tell me who you are. And if I don't like what I hear, I'll drop you off at the nearest police station."

He nods silently, blows out a breath before speaking. "My name is Leo Broz. I am twenty-one years old and until I met you, I was lost."

I knew this. This is something I had known for the past couple of hours but now I feel it. My chest tightens as do my fingers on the steering wheel, turning my knuckles white. "You lied to me. Why? Why did you even pretend to be him? I don't understand."

"I'm not sure. I just…" He pounds his fist on his knee before raking his hands through his hair. "I didn't plan to. I planned on coming to meet you as me, as Leo, but then I got scared. I came to the house twice and turned away, knowing I couldn't tell you the truth as it was."

"Why?"

"What was I supposed to say? That I had accidently killed the man who your aunt had sent? And expect you to welcome me in? I thought of telling you that day and every day since, but as soon as I saw you, being Max just seemed…"

"What?" I couldn't hold back my irritation any longer.

"Easier. I'd been wanting to forget my past so badly that it seemed destined to have the opportunity to do just that. It fell right into my lap. Like it was meant to be. And as soon as I saw you, it felt right."

I feel his eyes on me but I keep my gaze on the road.

"The funny thing is, after I got to know you I knew I didn't deserve you and at the same time that no one would love you the way that I could." He sighs. "And I still feel that way."

Pain. That's what I feel. Pain of betrayal, being made a fool of, not knowing what I should do because this man that I sit next to knows me better than anyone in the world and I feel as though I have no idea who he is. "I need you to start from the beginning. Every single thing. I have half a mind to kick you out of the car and not look back, so don't make me regret not doing it."

And for the first time, Leo speaks.

Chapter Thirty

Thirty minutes is spent in complete and utter silence. We don't even bother with the radio. Now is not the time for music. I'm processing, or at least trying to, everything he's told me. I want to believe him, but how do I? How do I know that what he says now is the truth when he's been lying for the past several months?

After checking in to the hotel, we walk silently to the room. The click of the lock settling into place seems to magnify the silence tenfold.

I lock myself in the bathroom for time to process. I need more time. Time is such a fickle thing. Never enough or too much. Pacing the floor in the tight space, I grow angrier as the minutes tick by. When I can't take it anymore, I swing the door open and march over to where Leo stands by the window.

"How dare you?" Before he can speak I push him.

His eyes widen and he raises his hands, palms out. "I'm so sorry. I didn't mean for it—"

It happens before I can think better of it and I reach up and slap him. A satisfying pain stings my hand and I shove him again. "I don't even know who you are!" I pound my fists against his chest and he doesn't stop me.

"You lied to me. How am I supposed to trust one word that comes out of your mouth? We're not even really married! How could you do this to me? Why?" He lets me hit him again and again until he finally grabs my wrists and pulls me closer.

He looks straight into my eyes and says, "You do know me. Everything you fell in love with is *me*. The only thing that's different is my name. You fell in love with *me*!" He slams his fist against his chest. "The love between us is not a lie." The sudden elevation in his emotions matches mine and he paces the floor with his hand clasped behind his neck. Just as quickly he's back in front of me, shouting, "Tell me you don't love me. You look at me and say you don't love me." The vein in his forehead throbs and I can't seem to drag my eyes down to meet his.

"I..." He scares me with his rage, but I'm too blinded by my own to back down. "I don't love you."

He takes my chin in his hand. "Look me in the eye and say you don't love me." His voice is hushed now, but still strained with emotion and intensity. "Say it."

I shake my head, tears running down my face. I can't do it.

One breath. It only takes one breath, one second of hesitation flashes in his eyes, before he kisses me in a way I never knew existed. It's tender and full of aching which makes me weep and forget and remember all at once. I forget the pain of moments ago and remember who he is. Who I fell in love with. And in this moment I realize it doesn't matter what his name is, what his past is. I get that the person I fell in love with was reinvented the day he met me, just as I was reinvented the day I met him. I never will be what I was before him nor him before me. That's what love does to people; disintegrates the two separate entities and gives birth to the joining of souls. So entwined they will never be the same as before.

The truth can give you everything you ever wanted and everything you never wanted at the same time. It feels like a punch to the gut to have all your suspicions validated and at the same time everything you dreaded, being put in your lap. Truth is a brutal, brutal thing.

Everything Leo's told me is still sinking in. My mind tries to make sense of it, grasp it, but it feels more like water slipping through my fingers.

I rush over to the suitcase and pull out the steel box. "Help me get this off." I tug at the lock, then put it on the ground and kick at it, desperate to find more truth.

"What are you doing? What is that?"

"Too many secrets in my life." Another kick. "It was my father's and I want to know what's in it." There's a feeling of spiraling that takes over. I feel like I'm losing my mind and all I can think about is getting the lock off.

"Just a second." Leo leaves and comes back a few minutes later carrying a tire iron from the car. He must be taking out some of the frustrations from the day because the lock pops off in less than a minute.

I've waited for years to find out what's in the box, knowing that whatever is in it holds something my father wanted to keep secret. Maybe something I need. My hands shake as I pick it up. I swing the lid open and feel somewhat disappointed with what I find: two keys. Defeated, I sink to my knees. "That's it? This is what I've tortured myself over all these years? Two lousy keys?" I wanted to find more. Something that might restore my scattered and threadbare memories. Something. Anything.

Leo picks them up and turns them over. "They look like safety deposit keys to me. See the numbers?" He holds them out so I can see the numbers etched into the metal. "We can check with the bank and go from there."

"Tomorrow?"

He shakes his head. "I don't know if we should go back to town while Max is still here. The keys don't seem like the most important thing in the world at the moment."

"Well, then what do you suppose we do? My life has been turned upside down and I want answers!" The sanity is leaving me. Everything feels so out of control and I can't grasp onto a single sane thought.

His voice softens. "I know. And we'll get them. We will find out where the keys go, but let's stop and think this through, okay? Let's figure out what to do about Max first."

I nod. "Do you think he'll just leave when I don't show up for dinner tonight?"

Leo stands and paces. "He came here to kill you. Even after he nearly died, he stayed in America. He came looking for you. And perhaps for me." He bites his thumb nail while pacing. "I bet that's exactly what he's after now. You *and* me. I just hope he doesn't realize he's found us both."

I watch him for a few moments, his brow furrowed and I realize how worried he is. "Come sit down for a minute."

He doesn't seem to hear me.

"Leo. Please, sit with me."

When his eyes connect with mine I see the panic. It sets my heart racing again, realizing he's truly afraid for our lives. "I can't let him get to you. Whatever the cost, he will never touch you."

I pat the spot on the bed next to me and he finally gives in and sits.

"You have to know that I believe with everything in my being that he will kill you. I've seen his soulless eyes. He's cruel and ugly and I can't let him get to you."

"I believe you."

"Can you trust me?"

I nod. Not sure if I fully believe it given everything that has happened, but it's something I want. And I truly have nothing else to lose at this point. I have to believe one of them and my gut says Leo is the man I need to trust.

When Leo speaks, there's a distance in his voice that worries me. "We need to lure him into a trap. Make him think he's meeting you, but really it's me waiting for him so I can take care of this once and for all."

Chapter Thirty-One

My nerves get the best of me as I pick up the phone. My palms are clammy so I wipe them on my dress before dialing the hotel's number.

"The Wellington Place Hotel. Good evening. How may I assist you?"

"I am expected to meet someone for dinner there in a few minutes and I won't be able to make it. I was wondering if he has arrived and if so, may I speak to him please? His name is Max Roth."

"Certainly. Hold for one moment please."

A moment or two passes before the hotel concierge is back. "Yes he just arrived. One moment while someone brings him to the telephone."

"Thank you." My heart thumps, picking up speed and force with each second that ticks by.

"This is Max Roth."

"Max. This is Gita. I am so very sorry, but I am not feeling well. I hate to do this since I postponed our meeting once already, but could we arrange to meet the day after tomorrow? I promise I will be there. You could come for dinner around seven o'clock at the house."

Silence for a beat. "Perhaps I could swing by right now. I could bring you dinner."

"That is so kind of you, but I'm actually at a friend's house for the night. I drove up to see her this afternoon, but fell ill. I have all the confidence in the world that I will be feeling much better in a couple of days."

"I guess I have no choice then but to wait. I've waited this long, what's a few more days?" The bitter in his voice cancels any attempt at cracking a joke and I worry that he knows something is going on.

"Thank you so much. I will see you Friday at the house then."

"See you then."

The line goes dead and I replace the receiver on the cradle.

"How did he seem?" Leo asks.

"Upset, but trying to hide it. Do you think he realizes something is going on?"

Leo nods. "It's possible. But let's stick to the plan and then this will all be behind us and we won't have to live life worrying about the past catching up to us any longer."

"That's just the thing though, the past always catches up."

~~~~

We drive through the night because neither one of us can sleep. I have so much going on in my head that it pounds and pounds making me sick to my stomach. "First stop is the bank. I need to see what is in the security boxes."

Leo keeps his eyes on the road, but nods. After breakfast at a diner, we go to the only bank in the fifteen mile radius of my house and wait for ten minutes before it opens. The wait is excruciating. I finger the keys, turning them over and over in my palm. Leo reaches over and stills my hands. "It's going to be okay."

As soon as the banker unlocks the doors, we get out of the car. I steal a glance around, scanning any passersby for Max's face. When we enter the bank we head straight for the teller.

"Good morning. May I help you?" The teller, a man about fifty years old peers at Leo over his spectacles.

But I'm the one who speaks. "I would like to see safety deposit boxes 61 and 62 please." I set the keys down on the counter.

"Right this way." He motions for me to follow him to a back room with a wall of locked boxes. "You may take the boxes in the room behind us for privacy."

I nod as he leaves us in front of the wall of steel containers.

Leo and I look at each other and he nods for me to go ahead. I slip the key in the first box. It unlatches and slips out of it cubby easily. I do the same for the second and we take them into the room, shutting the door behind us.

"Are you ready for this?" he asks.

"I think so." I lift the lid to the first one and find a stack of papers. Documents, passports, identification cards, birth certificates. I flip through them quickly, noticing names I don't recognize, before moving to the next box. There are more papers, but this has a stack a good half inch thick and is held together with a rubber band. My father's handwriting is scrawled across the front with the words "The Worth of a Soul."

"What is this?" I leaf through it not really reading anything.

"I'm not sure. Should we go ahead and take this and go through them at home?"

"Yes. This will take a while to go through it all."

We leave the bank with the stack of papers and head for home. As we approach our dirt road, we make sure there are no signs of Max. I'm paranoid that he'll be sitting on the porch waiting for me. Thankfully, we're alone.

Leo insists on going in the house first, but we find all is well and no disturbances. We spread the papers out on the kitchen table. The passports and identification papers don't make any sense. There are names on them and I recognize only three of more than a dozen. All the others are different.

"Why would my father have other people's documents?"

Leo shakes his head. "Maybe they are his. Yours."

"If we were on the run, that makes sense. But why would we keep our real names here if we went to all the trouble of changing them while running?"

He looks at me. "I don't think you would."

It clicks. The piece of that part of the puzzle snaps into place. "I remembered a conversation with my father and him telling me they would call me Gita. I was no longer to be…" A sudden wave of nausea pulses over me and I stand, letting the papers fall to the table. "This is too much. I don't know what to believe anymore."

"Gita. Maybe you should try to sleep. We've been up all night and this is a lot to take in all at once."

I don't say anything, just walk to the bathroom and turn on the shower. It feels like a safe place to break. I sink to the floor of the tub as the water streams down and I cry until I can't breathe and my ribs ache. I pound my fists on the side of the tub and feel too exhausted to face what I must.

"Gita." Leo's voice is gentle and hesitant like he's frightened. He pulls the shower curtain back and turns the now cold water off. I shake from the cold and I can't even muster enough strength to pick myself up and out of the tub.

"Come." He pulls me up, wraps a towel around my shivering shoulders and carries me to our bed. "Let's both just lie here awhile and get some rest. This will still be waiting for us when we wake up." The shivering eases as he wraps himself around me. It's the safest place I know.

Chapter Thirty-Two

I wake to the early afternoon sun coming in the window. Leo is gone. The sleep I did get has taken the edge off and I feel slightly more prepared to figure this all out. I find Leo sitting at the table reading the stack of papers. He looks up and attempts a smile. "I hope it's okay I looked at these."

"Of course." I sit next to him and lean over to see what it says.

"Gita, this is incredible. Your father was incredible."

"What does it say?"

"You need to read it for yourself. This is your father's account of the past twenty years. I wouldn't do it justice. Here." He slides the pile over to me and stands. "I'm going to give you some time to read. I'll be in the shower if you need me." He bends down and presses his lips to the top of my head. "I love you."

The words of my father, in his own handwriting, rattles me and I mourn for him all over again.

HEINZ AMSEL

The key to getting people to follow you is not telling them the whole truth. It's to make them think you are going to give them everything they want. Give them food, jobs, happiness that had been absent. Promise them a stronger, better country. It's all about the bait. Then once you have them on your side, take away choice. Keep filling them up with false promises and feed them full of lies and propaganda.

When Hitler first came into power, things were better. The economy improved from the First World War. Things were thriving in Germany. I was already in decent ranking in the German Army and it wasn't too long before I moved up. But even when I realized what I had become a part of, I had no choice but to do what was asked of me. I had my wife to think of and the rest of my family.

When I was assigned to Auschwitz, I nearly ran away. I had to leave my wife in Germany, only seeing her a couple times a month. At first we were bringing in prisoners, people who went against the party, but then the ghettos went up and pretty soon it wasn't enough. Hitler wanted the Jews to suffer more than having their food rationed and their possessions and livelihood taken. See, little by little. Evil doesn't win the hearts of men over night. It needs time to fester, take root, and grow. So that it can disguise itself as good at first and before you realize what's happening, it turns ugly. By then it's too late.

I'd be lying if I said that a little piece of me didn't die every time I went to work in the camp. Too much evil in one place does something to your soul if you're around it every day.

And then there was a moment that changed the way I looked at my position in the camp. Like most pivotal moments in our lives, it was but a brief instant where I saw a rare act of humanity. Something I could have easily missed or overlooked, but I didn't. I saw a fellow SS guard pull a piece of bread from his pocket and slip it to a young boy who was in line for the gas chamber. It was so subtle and quick, I questioned if I had even seen it.

That moment was the moment I realized maybe I was placed there in Auschwitz for a reason. If someone else had seen it, he would have been punished, perhaps even executed on the spot. Lucky for him, I was the only witness.

I kept an eye on the officer, a man named Oskar, and saw him do similar things. A piece of candy to a young boy. A hand up when no one was looking for an old man who was too fatigued to work. The typical thing to do was to beat him for not getting up on his own and working, not help him stand. It was a beautiful thing.

One day I went up to him in the courtyard when no other officers were within earshot and introduced myself. I glanced around before leaning closer saying, "I've seen how you treat the prisoners."

He stiffened and said, "I'm not sure I know what you mean."

"You're kind."

He shook his head, but I rushed to reassure him. "I think it's a good thing. You're a good man."

I caught his eyes flash to the right and I saw another officer approaching so I said nothing more to him that day. But a few days later when we were patrolling at night, he pulled me aside and said, "What exactly did you see me do?"

"I just saw you help a man up. And the food you gave to the boy. It's nothing to be ashamed of. I admire you. I do the same things when I can."

He nodded, still eyeing me. I suppose deciding if he could trust me.

From that time forward we became genuine friends. It wasn't too long before we came up with a plan to help even more. We asked to be put on Gas Chamber duty together; working with the Jewish prisoners we called Sonderkommandos. They were made to work in the gas chambers, cleaning out the bodies after the gassings, in exchange for slightly better accommodations. But their fate was sealed the day they were assigned because we only let them live for a short time. Usually three months or so, because they had such intimate knowledge of the camp and how it was run. There was a resistance that we worked with and on the days of small groups coming through, we would bring them in, take them out the back door directly onto a truck meant for loading personal items, like hair, gold fillings, that were taken from the dead before being put into the crematorium. We loaded them up and then took them to safe houses. We couldn't save everyone. Not even a large number, but I like to think the ones we did save made a difference and lived to tell that there was hope among the Hell.

It was risky to put it lightly. We would have been killed along with our families had the other officers found out. But we did it anyway, perhaps trying to save our sanity and human decency along with a few lives.

But one day changed everything.

I had been assigned night duty in one of the blocks where they kept the women. There was nothing unusual about that night. I had just stepped into one of the bunkhouses when I saw something on the floor partially under the bunk. I approached the object and shined my light on it and realized it was a small child. I crouched down, turning her over and my heart sank when I saw that she was dead. I wondered how she had even gotten through the first day when they usually sent small children to their death upon arrival for they were unable to be of use for labor.

I picked the girl up in my arms, she weighed nothing, and her bones felt paper thin like a bird. I couldn't stand the thought of her in the crematorium and I waited several moments, just holding her in the dark bunkhouse not knowing what to do.

And then she moved.

She looked dead, but ever so slightly her chest moved up and down, in and out. She was alive by some miracle. Without thinking, I wrapped her in a blanket and threw her over my shoulder. I walked like it was just another day and she was just another dead body, past several other officers toward the crematorium. The only good thing about the girl's near death circumstances was I knew she wasn't going to give us away with moving about or crying. When I got to the crematorium, as soon as no one was looking, I slipped passed it and went straight for my truck where I put her on the floor covered by the blanket. I knew she wouldn't be able to get up, so I wasn't worried so much about someone finding her as I was that she would be dead before I finished my shift.

A half of an hour ticked by and I couldn't stand it any longer. Running towards the latrine I passed my superior. I stopped to salute him and then said, "I'm going to be sick." So he waved me off. I made a good show of it until finally he told me to just go home since I only had an hour left in the shift anyhow.

When I got to the truck I didn't even look down at the lump on the floorboards. As soon as I was well out of the camp, I reached down and lifted the blanket a little so I could see her face. It was too hard to tell in the dark if she was still breathing. Punching down the accelerator, I drove until I reached my home in Germany.

Chapter Thirty-Three

My wife took one look at the girl and said, "What have you done?"

I shook my head and laid her down on the couch, then went and drew the blinds. "I couldn't just leave her there. They would have killed her."

She sighed, and went to the kitchen for a rag and a bowl of water. "She looks good as dead." I watched as my wife tenderly wiped the child down, cleaning her as best she could with a rag. "She needs to eat. Look at her. She's nothing but skin and bones."

I fetched some water from the tap and brought it to my wife. "Let's sit her up and I'll see if she can drink it. If she doesn't…" She shook her head. Putting the spoon to her lips, she gave the girl a few drops of water. At first it just ran out of her mouth, then she seemed to stir and began choking on it.

"That's good for now. Let her rest," I said.

After placing a blanket over her, I followed my wife into the kitchen. "What happened to her anyway? How did you become involved?"

I ran a hand over my head, not knowing how much to divulge. "I saw her lying in a heap on the floor next to a bunk. I don't know how she got there because the little ones usually don't make it past—"

My wife held up her hand to stop me. "Please, I can't hear anymore. How did you get her out?"

I relayed the evening to her and when I was done she said, "What are you planning on doing with her?"

I looked at her straight in the eyes and she knew. "You can't keep her. She has a family."

"I don't think she does. I think I remember her from her arrival day. Her mother kept her close and somehow she convinced the officer to let her stay with her. The officer probably did knowing that they would both be sent to the gas chambers soon anyway. I remember her mother. I remembered her. I looked for her when I did bunker patrols and never saw her so I think her mother must have hidden her under the bunk and kept her there. I'm not sure what happened to the mother, but I'll look when I go to work tomorrow."

"If we keep her, how do we go about that? Growing up in hiding is no life for a child."

"I intend to run."

My wife put her head down and cried, knowing it's what we should do, but hating the thought of leaving her family and home.

"Fran, we must. I was meant to find her. I know I was."

She reached out and patted my hand. "I know. I just pray we aren't signing our death orders."

~~~~

The next day I headed back to the camp where I looked for the girl's mother. I woke a lady who lay near where I found the girl, "Where is the woman with the little girl?"

"I don't know."

"You know who I speak of though, don't you? The little girl that stayed in here."

Her eyes grew wide. "We told her the child would get her killed, but she didn't listen. We didn't help her, I promise. She's gone anyway. They both are."

"You're not in trouble. I just want to find the mother."

"She wasn't the mother. The woman brought her here when she was transferred from another camp. She said she has promised the mother she would take care of her, but the woman had gone mad. She had lost all common sense, keeping that girl under the bunk even while she was so sick she couldn't eat. An officer took her the other day and she never returned. She had been ill, not able to get out of bed herself."

"And the girl? You said she was gone as well." My heart thrummed in my chest, hoping she didn't see me take her the night before.

"She was gone when I woke up this morning."

I left without worrying about taking a child from her mother. I knew it must have been as I suspected and had no qualms about taking the child with me on the run. If she survived.

Chapter Thirty-Four

I had to find a way to leave without raising suspicion for a few days. When I spotted Oskar at our lunch break, I called him over.

"I'm leaving," I whispered.

"How. When?"

"Soon. I haven't figured it all out yet, but I need to be quick about it."

He sat, staring at the ground. "I wish I could come with you. But I can't. And there aren't enough people to trust here." His eyes shifted around the room. "Where will you go?"

"I don't know. The war must end sometime, right? I hope to come back when it's safe."

"You'll never be able to return, my friend. When they find out you crossed them, they will never allow you to come back without killing you and your family."

The thought made me pause, realizing he was right and how hurt Fran would be.

"What can I do to help?"

"I need a few days off to get a heads start. Could you cover for me?"

"I already work. You could ask Hans. He isn't working."

"Do you think he'll suspect anything?"

Oskar shook his head. "Nothing wrong with taking a few days off. Especially if you're sick."

We stood and I clasped my hand on his shoulder. "You're a good man, Oskar. And a good friend."

"The same to you. I wish you could stay, but I admire your bravery. I wish you well."

I couldn't let the other officers around know we were saying goodbyes or else when I was gone, the wrath would come down on Oskar's head. So we made it quick and went back to work.

I approached Hans at the end of my shift, clutching my stomach.

His brows furrowed, "Are you sick again?"

I nodded, "I can't seem to shake this. I'm weak and can't stop running to the latrine so I need to take a few days off. Could you take my shift for the weekend?"

"Sure. If you take a couple days for me next week."

"If I'm feeling better, I'll be happy to. You're a good man. Will you let the boss know?"

"Sure. Feel better."

The minute I got out of sight of the camp, I went fast and didn't stop until Fran, the child, and I were safe at my sister's house in Lobau, Germany.

~~~~

Frieda opened the door and her face went from surprise to seeing us to confusion when her eyes fell on the blanket-swaddled child in my arms.

I pushed past her, not waiting for an invitation.

"Heinz, who is that? What's all this about?"

Fran rushed to shut all curtains as I went to the bedroom in the back with Frieda on my heels. "Tell me what is happening."

"The less you know, the better." I laid the girl on the bed, who stirred briefly then went still again. "Can you get me some water please? And a spoon?"

"Well, if you tell me what's going on, maybe I will. You storm into my house in the middle of the night and can't tell me what's going on. I feel I at least—"

"I will tell you, but I need the water. Now!" My voice was hushed, but I left no room for arguing. Our eyes met until I saw we'd reached an understanding.

Hurried exchanges from Frieda and Fran filled the silence as I unwrapped the girl from the blanket cocoon and rearranged it on top of her.

We made quick work of attempting to get some water down her, but most of it ended up rolling down her chin and pooling on her shirt. "Come now, you must take this," Fran said as she rubbed the girl's back. "One sip now." The girl was nonresponsive for the most part but seemed agitated, so Fran rubbed harder. "Wake now. Drink." The girl's mouth moved slightly as the spoon pushed past her lips and her head turned to the water.

The child's lips were cracked. Her tongue was white and swollen from dehydration. There was little life left in her and I worried it wouldn't be enough to make it through the night. I'd seen some horrifying things in the camp and it always surprised me when the ones who looked like they had already died rose up again and again to keep going. The will to live is stronger in some and I realized I must find that in the girl.

I took the spoon from my wife's hand and said to the girl, "You are safe now. Drink. You are safe." I rubbed her back softly, afraid of hurting her frail body and whispered. "Now is not the time to give up. That would have been several days ago. This is the time to fight, my girl. Fight."

She coughed as her throat tried to remember how to swallow and I figure it was all we could do for the moment. We laid her back down and got her as comfortable as we could before stepping to the corner of the room to talk.

Frieda looked at me, some sort of emotion that I couldn't identify passed over her face. "What have you done?" Then, turning to Fran, "Someone better tell me what is going on."

"Like I said earlier, the less you know the better. But I will say this, we are leaving Germany. We need to stay here for a few days until the girl is well enough to travel and then we will leave. If you don't want us here, I will understand."

A beat passed with Fran and me looking at her before she responded. "You can stay. But I want more answers."

I shook my head. "I can't give you any. You have to know it's for your safety. If they come looking for us I don't want—"

Frieda's hand flew up. "Who? Who will be looking for you? I'm sure you aren't speaking of the SS?" When I didn't speak she cursed under her breath. "And you plan on running away and never coming home? I will never see you again, little brother?"

I pleaded with her, trying to convince her that this was the only way. I had no choice at that point. "I will come home one day. This can't go on forever. This country that I love...I can't bear to think of it. When a good amount of time has passed I am hopeful we can return again. I will write to you when I feel it's safe. But until then, you mustn't know any specifics."

What I asked her to do was enough to get her killed. She knew it, we all knew it. The quiet settled over us like a dark cloud and I jumped when the girl coughed. We glanced over at the child, before our eyes met again and with a nod from Frieda, we went back to tending to the girl.

~~~~

We spent the rest of the night and into the late morning spoon feeding the child water and broth. She became more alert, though still lethargic, but at least her body responded by accepting the liquid. We did it slowly; just a spoonful every twenty minutes, then gradually increased it to two spoonsful. We crushed up aspirin to bring down her fever and my wife kept a cool rag on her forehead. Frieda and I both spent many moments at the curtained windows, pulling them back and letting them fall just as quickly.

I can't lie. There were many times I wondered if I had done the right thing, taking the girl. I have never regretted saving her life, but taking her to my family, risking their lives, is what gave me pause.

The night brought the child out of her lethargy slightly. She opened her eyes and said, "Drink." Her voice, so tiny and sweet like the call of a bird.

Fran's eyes stayed on the child, but I saw tears as she spoke. "Here, little one." She raised the cup to the child's lips and smoothed down her hair in such a maternal way that made a lump form in my throat. It was at that moment that I realized she felt as attached to the girl then as I did and she would never regret my bringing her there.

Chapter Thirty-Five

After a couple of long, sleepless nights I reported back to work. It was important for me to act naturally and go about business as usual for as long as I could until the girl was strong enough to travel. No boat would allow a sick child onboard.

The day matched my mood. Low, dark clouds hung in the sky, drizzling on and off. The soft pitter patter of rain on the roofs made a somber song to the dance of the camp. The ugly, horrifying dance of Nazis pushing and shoving. Men marching, working. There should never be a sunny day in a place like that.

The moment Oskar saw me, his eyes grew wide and I knew he was wondering why I was there. "Meet me around the building in a minute," I whispered as we passed each other.

It took more than a minute for him to arrive. I grew nervous wondering if I could trust him. What was taking him so long? I only had a minute left before I needed to be back at my post. Just before accepting he wasn't coming, he rounded the corner.

"What are you doing here?"

"I needed more time." I glanced over his shoulder, making sure no one could see us.

"You are playing a dangerous game, my friend. If you stay much longer, you'll put everyone in danger."

I nodded, knowing he spoke the truth. "I need your help. Can you get us passports? I know you have access to some in the SS command. I need one for myself, Fran, and a little girl."

His eyes widened, knowing I had no children. He shifted, looked around before nodding. "They'll be waiting for you here at the end of my shift. Don't be late. I don't want anyone happening upon them."

I took him by the shoulders and looked in his eyes. "Thank you, brother. You will be blessed for this."

We hugged before rushing off to our posts.

The day dragged on. I wondered how the girl was. My mind remained at my sister's house where I wondered if they were alright. I would need to spend another day or so here before traveling back to Frieda's house. I just hoped the missing documents wouldn't be noticed until then.

Towards the end of my shift, I walked outside. I couldn't help myself from glancing at the building, wondering if the papers were there. I looked over and saw Oskar laughing with another officer just a few yards away. We made eye contact and he gave the slightest of nods before turning back to the other man. I waited for his back to be turned before I crept up to the building. Just as I did, another guard called out to me.

"Halt!"

Panic raced through my veins, pumping so loudly in my ears I felt I wouldn't be able to hear.

I turned to see a guard I didn't recognize rushing towards me. My heart gave way to the sheer fear I felt in that moment. It wasn't until he had passed me that I realized he was speaking to someone else.

Sweat soaked through my shirt even though it was chilly out. I needed to get it together because anyone that laid eyes on me would know something was wrong. I felt like I wore my crimes on my forehead that anyone looking at me could plainly see. Dabbing at the perspiration on my upper lip with a handkerchief, I made my way to the back of the building. I didn't see anything.

I frantically rushed about, searching for them, doubt creeping in again about Oskar's trustworthiness. Then I saw an envelope sidled up flush against the wall half buried in the dirt. Only one looking for it would find it.

I wasted no time before shoving it inside my coat pocket and heading straight to my truck. My heart pounded as I was stopped at the gate by the guards as was routinely done, and didn't stop pounding until I was far away from the camp.

I wanted to get to my family. But I knew I couldn't. I wouldn't have time to drive there and back before my shift started in another six hours. The drive is at least four hours each way. I would have to try to sleep, though I knew I wouldn't be able to.

~~~~

Steam rose from the cup of coffee in front of me and I watched in a daze. Fatigue was kicking in and making me more and more paranoid. I had tried sleeping briefly only to start every time I heard a noise, sure it was the Furor himself coming for me. I finally gave up and decided if I wasn't going to be able to sleep, I should try and stay alert.

For three hours I sat at the kitchen table, sipping cup after cup of coffee.

When the time came to go to work, my hands shook from the caffeine. I glanced in the rearview mirror and saw how the dark circles under my eyes gave away my fatigue.

"Morning." An SS guard saluted as I passed. I gave my solute back and carried on.

It was another grim, cold, gray day and the smoke from the bunker rose to meet its gray sisters of the clouds.

I looked for Oskar throughout the morning but never found him. Lunch came and he wasn't eating. Towards the end of the day, I stopped Hans as we passed. "Have you seen Oskar today?"

"Keine. He didn't show up. Someone said he was feeling sick last night before he left. You okay?" He eyed me up and down. "You look like you might still be sick too."

"I've been fighting something for a week or so. But I'm fine."

He eyed me again, "You still want me to cover for you?"

"Actually, that might be for the best. I thought I was getting better, but I guess not. Will tomorrow and the next day be okay?"

He nodded before continuing on.

I wondered if Oskar was okay, because something seemed off.

~~~~

I couldn't take it anymore. Being away from my family, not knowing if they were okay. I would have called, but my sister didn't have her own telephone. And the fact that I couldn't get ahold of them was making me crazier than the paranoia.

I packed up very few basic things and took one last look around. The sight of my wife's china that had been given to her by her grandmother sent a shot of guilt through me. I knew this would be hard for Fran. Leaving our friends, our loved ones, our home and all the memories we had here. But there was no other choice now. The longer I dwelt on it, the sooner someone would catch up to us. I knew once I walked out that door, the clock was ticking and it would only be a matter of time before someone found out what I had done.

On the drive to Frieda's, I wondered why no one had said anything about the girl who had gone missing. Then I remembered that she had never been accounted for, having been hidden by the woman under the bunk.

My heart broke for her mother, her father, even the woman who had kept her, who never survived long enough to see the girl free.

~~~~

Two hours and thirty-five minutes. That's how long it took us to leave Frieda's home.

We waited for the comfort of darkness before loading the truck up with our very few possessions and a lump of a blanket that held the girl.

We drove fast, only stopping to refill the tank of gasoline with the gas cans I had brought. There was no going back now. We spoke little, afraid of waking the girl or maybe afraid of bringing bad luck upon us if we spoke of what we were doing. It was easier than I thought, crossing into France. The girl had become stronger while I was away. She had been bathed and had been able to take more broth, speaking more, but still very little.

A whisper from Fran broke the quiet. "She asked for her mother when she woke up this morning. She was looking at me with those eyes and I didn't know what to tell her. She wasn't quite awake enough to understand anyway, so it probably didn't matter what I said. She was more asking for her mother because she wanted comfort. But still…"

The silence stretched between us in the darkness of the truck as we bounced along a torn-up road. "So what did you say?"

"I said, 'I'm right here.'"

My wife's cries were more felt than heard. In an attempt to comfort her, I reached over the sleeping child and took her hand in mine.

Chapter Thirty-Six

I wonder sometimes if all the bad deeds one does in their life are ever erased by the good ones they do. There were things I didn't want to do, but I had to do them. I sometimes cursed myself for not leaving the regime sooner, but then always went back to knowing there was a reason I was there on that day to find the girl.

Two days we spent driving until we made it to the port. The ship looked like it might fall apart at any time and was filled with too many people, but somehow it stayed afloat. It took us a couple of weeks to reach America. And those are a couple of weeks I try to forget.

When we finally reached the States, we headed south to West Virginia. I had heard from another passenger on the boat that there were farms there and it seemed like the perfect place to hide. Somewhere we could plant our own food, sell things for income. I had money and gold bars stuffed in my pants and in a satchel that I never took off. It was a significant amount that I had taken off the hands of two of the commanding officers. I knew it was dirty money anyway, being taken from the Jews. So I had no problem taking it from them. Though I vowed to somehow pay it back someday.

It was three days on American soil when we found a rundown farmhouse with a land that had been let go. And it was four days later our little girl really showed signs of improvement. Holding down regular food. Staying awake for longer than a half hour at a time. She was shy and didn't want to speak. Every time I spoke to her, she shrunk behind her mother's arm.

"Don't you want to see what I have for you?" I held out my hands, fists closed. She sat on the bed and just stared at me. She had yet to gift me with her words or a smile. "Pick a hand and see if there's something for you."

She tentatively reached out and with her little finger, tapped on my right hand. I flipped it over, opening it up to reveal a piece of candy. "Go ahead. It's yours."

I held it out to her and the corner of her mouth came up as she reached for it. It was the next day she gave me a hug and took my heart.

~~~~

Days passed with Fran, me and the girl working on the farm. Tilling the land, planting a large garden in the spring. A haphazard orchard of fruit and black walnut trees were already at maturity, but needed pruning. We spent days in the sun planting, picking, harvesting and selling what extras we had. We kept to ourselves, not wanting too many questions and it was easy to do. The people of our small town grew weary of us as German emigrants. No one stopped by. We never had anyone over for a cup of coffee or tea. When we went to town, we spoke little as our English was very broken, and the storekeepers said just as few words back to us.

The only people we ever spoke to more than a few times was the older couple who lived across the field. Every now and then one of the Henderson's cows would get out and into our property and I would have to return it. They were a nice couple who also kept to themselves quite a bit and took an immediate liking to our daughter. Which was all the more reason to keep our distance from them.

One night after Fran came in from hanging clothes on the line she said, "The Hendersons were asking about her again today. Asked how she got those beautiful hazel eyes. I'm sure she meant nothing of it, but it felt like she was accusing us. The way that woman carries on sometimes and then just sits and stares other times…There's something wrong with her."

"We should just keep to ourselves then. Better for everyone. Anyway, I'm afraid one day Gita will remember something and what if she slips up in front of someone? What if she confides in the wrong person? We can't have that. It's best to keep to ourselves from now on."

Fran nodded but I saw a fleeting look of sadness in her eyes before she walked out of the kitchen. Another ripple of guilt rolled through my chest realizing all that she had given up because of my decision. She no longer had family and now I was asking her to not make friends. It wasn't fair to her and yet, she never complained.

~~~~

It was nearly two years after we arrived that the war ended. I thought perhaps the people in the spread out farming town might not worry about us so much anymore, but I took no chances. I wish I could say the paranoia that the Nazi party was still looking for me eased as well, but it didn't. There was so much happening in Germany at that point, I figured no one was worrying about me. If they hadn't tracked me down in two years, I couldn't imagine they would do so now and yet a nagging persisted.

But then a new problem presented itself. One day I sat, listening to the news on the radio when Gita walked in. "Do you know a boy name Josef?"

I tipped my head to the side, wondering where this was coming from. "I don't believe so. Why?"

She traced a circle on the couch with her thumb, eyes intent on watching it go around and back and forth. Finally she spoke again, "I just keep thinking of a boy in the back of a truck and him handing me a blanket. And then I remember crying for a boy named Josef."

My mouth went dry and I couldn't seem to find words. She had begun to remember. I panicked, not knowing what the right thing to do was. I wanted to tell her the truth; she had a right to know after all. But something stopped me. Maybe it was her age. She was so innocent. Even after all she had been through, her heart remained untainted from the world. And I wanted to keep her that way. "It must have been a dream long ago. Now go see if you can help your mother with dinner."

Her brows furrowed, but she did as I said and left the room. She would come to me several times over the next few years with questions. I felt the more I reassured her they were just her wild imagination, then perhaps she would stop.

She never did.

~~~~

After the war ended we finally contacted Frieda. We kept our new names, the ones we had stolen, so that no one would know it was us. Even though I knew we were in the clear, I was still a bit paranoid. Two weeks after sending the initial letter, she wrote back, thrilled to hear from us.

Dear Mr. Amsel,

You can't imagine the amount of relief I feel from receiving your letter. I am well and in good health and hope you are as well. There was a brief time when my brother went missing that men would come around asking all sorts of questions. They thought they intimidated me, but they didn't realize who they were dealing with. I haven't heard from them in over a year

*and don't expect to. I wish I could see my brother again,
but I fear he is dead. And that's just what I told the
officers. That I believe he and his wife jumped off the
bridge after the grief of not being able to bare children
became too much for them. I even showed them the short
note he had left explaining what they were going to do.
Please write again soon. I want to hear all about your
wife and daughter.*

    Love,
    Frieda

I can't describe the amount of relief I felt when I
got that letter. It was truly a weight off my shoulders
when I heard she was okay. Alive. Something in me
seemed to calm from that day on. I was no longer
startling awake at night. I stopped looking for the eyes
of SS soldiers from my past. The load of bricks I had
been carrying around seemed to have dropped from my
back and I was a lighter man because of it.

GITA
1952

Chapter Thirty-Seven

I shed no tears until I put the last page down. And then I sob and weep and shake with sadness that he's no longer here. That my mother is no longer here. Then I get angry that they never told me the truth. I know they were scared, but I was no longer a child. There were so many chances they could have told me. So many opportunities I gave them. So many thoughts roar through my head like an enormous, angry ocean wave.

After I allow myself to feel the entirety of the emotions, when all is said and done, there is no way I couldn't be more grateful for my parents and the sacrifices they made because of a little girl. Me. The love they had for me, a stranger, to risk their lives, never to see their families again. Never to set foot on the soil of their home country they loved. I feel so undeserving and yet incredibly special.

With this new information and my new identity I feel as though I need to mourn not only the loss of my parents, but of the family I surely had but with no recollection. I need to mourn the loss of so many of my people.

Leo stands in the doorway, and I'm not sure how long he's been there. When I look at his face, I see him for the first time. "That's why I felt you were like home to me. Because you are."

He knows exactly what I'm saying. We've survived the same Hell. He crosses the room and I stand to meet him as he wraps his arms around me. The strength of them buoys me up and I feel that the two of us can do anything.

I whisper against his chest, "Will you help me remember who I am?"

~~~~

I tip my head back against the headboard and close my eyes. "I still have so many questions." Each time I cry, the throbbing in my head pounds harder, fiercer.

Leo scoots over to me on the bed and pulls me to him. I curl up and let him hold me. "Shhh. You have had too much today. Try to get some sleep so we can think more clearly tomorrow. We have to be ready to face Max."

The thought of tomorrow coming is nearly impossible to embrace. I just want it all over. I want Max to be gone and Leo and I on the farm living the rest of our lives in peace. But even now in my foggy, emotionally-drained state, I know it won't be that easy.

The night is spent in a dreamless sleep. I know Leo is having just as hard of a time sleeping because every time I awake to toss and turn, he's fidgeting as well.

I listen as the faucet in the bathroom drips. Every six seconds. Drip. One, two, three, four, five, drip.

Darkness still shrouds us when he says, "I can't sleep." His fingers trail up the back of my arm. "My past is catching up with me and it brings nightmares with it."

I roll over so our faces are only inches away from each other. "I suppose you think me lucky that I can't remember."

"At times. There are times when I'd do anything to forget. But then I'd forget my family and that would be more of a tragedy than remembering the horror of it all."

That's when the ache sets in. It starts in my chest and works its way to my belly, settling in, gripping me. There were parents, maybe siblings that I once loved and I can't even remember them. Can't bring up an image of a face anytime I want.

Josef.

"I think I had a brother."

"Are you remembering something?"

"Well, I've always remembered some things. Bits and pieces. The boy in the truck with the blanket. I just have a feeling…There's too much emotion connected to that memory. I remember crying for him."

Somberness enters the room and lays its heavy self over us, weighing us down. "I don't even know what to call myself now. I remember Lidka. I remember a conversation anyway about not being able to be called by that name anymore. I feel kind of robbed. I didn't get a chance to know who she was."

"You're still the same person."

I shake my head. "No I'm not. But I guess I'll just have to come to terms with that. It feels weird though, because I'm not sure what the right thing is. If I should go by the name that my birth parents gave me or go by the name I've know most of my life and that was given to me by the people who saved my life."

"I guess you'll know when the time is right if you decide to go by Lidka. It's a beautiful name. It fits you." Another long stretch of silence before he says, "You realize we were at the same camp? He saved us both."

I prop myself up on my elbow. "Are you sure?"

In a swift, gentle movement he moves the hair from my face. "If your father saved you from the camp he worked at and he saved me as well, then we must have been. It also explains the connection I felt towards you immediately. You are home to me as well."

The night gives us a false sense of safety, like we can say anything here and our secrets will be kept safe. Things we could never say in the daylight, too exposed.

"I will forever be thankful to your father for saving us. It must have been God's plan for us, because what are the chances of being saved by the same man, coming to America and falling in love? There's no doubt in my mind our souls were designed for each other. I don't believe in happenstance."

I realize he's right and my chest swells. Too many pieces of the puzzle coming together in a way that couldn't be chance. Many times over the past few months I had longed for my father to have met Leo. And now that I know he had, I'm ripped apart and put back together again and I long for Leo to be that vise keeping all the pieces of me together.

"Will you say some of your poems to me? Maybe it will help us both keep our minds off of the sadness. Because right now the grief of missing my parents and the parents I can't remember is just too overwhelming. Hold me tighter. Please."

I settle in with his arms secured tightly around me as his breath tickles the nape of my neck and his words distract me. Though his lips that brush against my skin rival his words in holding my attention.

> *"How do I love thee? Let me count the ways.*
> *I love thee to the depth and breadth and height*
> *My soul can reach, when feeling out of sight*
> *For the ends of being and ideal grace.*
> *I love thee to the level of every day's*
> *Most quiet need, by sun and candle-light.*
> *I love thee freely, as men strive for right;*
> *I love thee purely, as they turn from praise.*
> *I love thee with the passion put to use*
> *In my old griefs, and with my childhood's faith.*
> *I love thee with a love I seemed to lose*
> *With my lost saints. I love thee with the breath,*

Smiles, tears, of all my life; and, if God choose,
I shall but love thee better after death."

"Did you write that?"

He shakes his head. "Elizabeth Barrett Browning."

"Do one of yours."

Moments pass before he speaks again.

"The darkened night stole you.

It was the men that separated us, but it was the darkness of the night that ripped away the sight of you.

Your face is nearly gone from my mind. Not even in print does it exist.

When I learned what it was, I watched the heaven-bound smoke as it reached up up up, afraid I had missed your turn. Had missed my last goodbyes. With the smoke of you.

You said we would find each other. Not to worry.

You lied.

I pretended you were still alive, that the men, the night, the smoke didn't take you. It was my turn to lie."

I feel as though my heart has been ripped out. I go to tell him to stop, but know it's his way of grieving. "Who is that about?"

"My mother."

My voice breaks when I say, "Say another."

"The hushed goodbyes in the dead of night

Left us both longing for more

But the cresting sun pulled me away from your embrace

And into a coming storm

One last kiss and another still,

Tested my resolve to depart

I wish I could say I would have professed my love

That I would have given you my heart

But that would be nothing more than empty words

A promise that could not be bound

For what I longed for most was nothing you could give

Because true love I had not yet found."

His thumb traces invisible circles on my wrists as he speaks. "I'm not quite sure it's finished."

I nod in the darkness. "Was it about someone you…" Suddenly I feel as though I'm prying, not sure I want to know the answer.

"It's about a girl in Germany who I wished I could have loved because she deserved it. But I didn't and so I left."

"You are good at leaving aren't you?"

His thumb stops. "I was. Until I met you."

"Will you stay? Or will the restless side of you catch up eventually? I need to know because I can't go through another loss."

He gets up so he's kneeling on the bed, bent over me. Taking my face in his hands he says, "The only reason I was restless and always on the run was because I was searching for something. You are that something. The need to run is gone. I told you, the minute I found you I knew you were the one I was looking for my entire life. You felt it too. There is nothing else I need in life more than you. You are all I have and all I want."

Chapter Thirty-Eight

We never did fall to sleep but got up with the sun and dressed as if we had some place we needed to be. "We need to go over the plan again. If it doesn't work…" I shake my head in an attempt to chase away the thought. "I just can't live running for the rest of my life."

"We won't. It will work and we will move on. I've wandered for too long."

"Are you sure this is the only way?"

He shifts his gaze to the window. "You know he came to take everything you have and then kill you. And he wants nothing more than to kill me. If he knew I was here, if he hasn't figured it out already, he wouldn't hesitate to kill me. So if it means keeping you safe, I will kill him."

"Why don't we just go to the police?"

"And say what? He's done nothing illegal here."

I sigh, too tired to think about it. "Maybe we'll have to wait until he comes to the house and then call the police, say he's trespassing."

"You think that he won't come back when the police are gone? He's out for revenge. He won't be

stopped. If you heard the things he said on the boat…"
Leo's voice strains to stay quiet.

The fear creeps in again when I realize he's right.
My mind spins and the air is getting harder and harder to
breathe.

He crouches down in front of me and his touch
immediately calms me. "Everything is going to be fine.
We'll make it. I will keep you safe. You are going to
have to trust me though. Which I know is a lot to ask for
after everything. If you can't trust me, trust your gut.
Listen to what it's telling you." He nods, keeping eye
contact. I must agree because I nod along with him.
"Good. Now we wait."

~~~~

The next couple hours I spend doing everyday things
with the hyperaware sense in the back of my mind that
this is very much not an ordinary day. The wind blows a
small tree limb across the dry grass and shakes the few
remaining leaves from their branches. The clouds roll in,
but no rain falls. The wind blows and howls and creates
noise in the otherwise noiseless house. Leo stays close,
but keeps busy watching out the windows every few
minutes.

"Want to eat?" I ask as I put the last of the dishes in
the cupboard.

"I'm not hungry. You told him to be here at seven
tonight, right?" Leo's leg bounces up and down so hard
it shakes the table.

"Yes. You were there when I called him."

"I know. I just have a feeling this isn't going to go as we expect it. That something is not right."

"Leo, I've been thinking. Can we please just try and get him to leave before we go to such extreme measures? We have had too much killing and death in our lives." The more I think about what he wants to do, the sicker I become. I don't want to be like Max.

"We will talk to him first, but if he leaves me no other choice…" His eyes soften. "I don't want more killing either. I hope it won't come to that, but I know him and what he's capable of. And I will do anything to keep you safe. Anything."

I glance at the clock. 5:37. We still have a little over an hour before he'll be here and I have no idea what to do with myself.

Leo stands suddenly. "We need to have your father's gun loaded just in case. Where did you say the other bullets were?"

"Out in the barn on the shelf above the garden tools." A shudder makes it way up my spine. I hate the thought of us even having a chance to use them.

"I'll be right back." He makes eye contact to see if I'm okay, so I nod.

I make my way to the front of the house in the living room. The storm has rushed dusk and it's getting dark inside the house. I switch the lamp on, but then think better of it and turn it off so I can peek out the window. Drawing the curtain back, I don't see much.

The porch light reaches just to the edge of the lawn. Shadows play across the dead grass as the wind blows the branches of the trees, making the light and shadows go back and forth in a dance with one another.

"Looking for someone." Before I can react, a strong arm wraps around my body, pinning my arms down to my sides. "Where is he?" Max hisses in a thick German accent. I feel something hard dig into my back. "Tell me where he is. I know he's here. If you tell me, I'll let you live for a little longer. And if you scream I will blow your brains out right now."

I shake my head, my voice paralyzed by fear.

His grip tightens as the cold metal digs harder into my skin. I close my eyes, not wanting this to be real.

"Fine. If you don't want to talk, I'll find a way to make you." He spins me around, pulls out a roll of tape and stretches it over my mouth. Grabbing my cheeks with one hand he leans in close to my ear. "You will pay for killing my father. You will pay and it will be a hefty fee. You will wish you were never born. I will have you begging for your life. It's because of you my father was killed and it's time someone pay for it."

He drags me to the bedroom where he shoves me on the ground, then makes quick work of binding my hands together with duct tape. He rips the pillow out of its case and yanks it over my head, wrapping the tape around the pillowcase, synching it at my neck. "Stay here and stay quiet or you can watch me kill him too."

Terror consumes me when the door clicks shut. I hear nothing except the pouring rain outside the window I lie under. Then I hear Leo.

"Gita? Where did you go?"

Despite Max's warning, I try to yell through the tape and the fabric. I know he can't hear me though. I suck air through the fabric pressed against my face, but it's growing heavier and hotter and panic fills me up. There's a part of me telling me it's okay that I can still breathe through my nose, to slow down, calm down. I can't. My chest heaves in and out picking up speed until I feel dizzy. I struggle to stand, but finally get to my feet where I sway, the dark and my panic making it hard to keep balance. I fall once against the side of the bed, smacking my head on the bed post. The dizziness increases and I try to stand again, only to fall to the ground once more. Air is near nonexistent now. My lungs can't get the oxygen they need and I finally just let go.

LEO

Chapter Thirty-Nine

The minute I step into the house I feel it. The energy has changed and something is wrong. "Gita. Where are you?" I check the kitchen. Not there. I'm dripping wet from being outside in the storm where I searched for the bullets to Gita's dad's gun. I glance down the hall and see the bathroom door is open with the light off, so I know she's not there. "Gita? Are you sure the bullets are in the barn? I couldn't find them." Still no answer. I walk into the living room and flip on the light.

"You mean these?" Max sits in the chair with the shotgun across his lap, and a handful of bullets on display.

My body freezes. "Where's Gita?"

He slips the bullets into his jacket pocket as he stands, gun pointed at me. "You don't act surprised to see me. You thought I was dead after all. So why don't you looked more surprised?"

"What do you want?" I try to keep him talking while I figure out what to do about finding Gita.

"Vengeance. Eye for an eye. Her father got my father killed. You tried to kill me and then come and take what's mine. You dirty scum. Did you have this planned from the time you got on the boat? That you could just get rid of me and take what wasn't yours? It's a brilliant plan really. But what I don't get is what a guy like you would want with a dirty Jew?" He takes a step closer as he speaks. "Unless of course, you aren't who you told me you were."

"Where is she?"

His eyes narrow and he tilts his head. "You actually care about her." Another step closer.

I keep my eyes on his, but try to keep tabs on the muzzle of the shotgun as well.

"I didn't expect that. I must say. When I fell overboard, I was lucky enough to find a piece of driftwood that I clung to until I was rescued. I was in pretty rough shape and it took me quite a while to get out of the hospital. Then I had to contact people back home and ask them to find out where Gita lived. It took many false tries before we found her, but it was worth it. Because then I saw you and it was like my father was leading me straight to you and her. Killing two birds with one stone, as they say. And I'll be back on a boat to Germany before anyone even finds you. It's quite perfect, really, because you both are such loners with no family and no one to miss you. Nobody will even find you for a while. Perfect."

The muzzle of the gun is within two feet of my reach. If I lunged for it I might be able to grab it. My heart pounds and time slows down.

"I think I want her to watch though. Let's go get—"

Before he can finish, I lunge forward and off to the side, grabbing the barrel and pointing it up at the ceiling. It goes off and plaster rains down around us.

We struggle for a few moments before I'm able to knock the gun out of his hands. I punch him, once, twice, three times before he is able to hit me on the side of my head. My ears ring and I lose focus for a second, giving him enough time to get up on his feet.

I shake my head trying to gain focus back into my vision and reach for the gun before he can get to it. I aim at his forehead. "Take me to her."

When he doesn't move I yell, "Now!"

We pass the bathroom and make our way to the bedroom. "Open it." I encourage him by pressing the barrel into his back. He tries opening the door, but something is stopping it. Shoving him out of the way, I put my shoulder against the door, pushing it harder until it gives enough for us to fit through the opening. I shove him in before me, keeping ahold of his shirt, afraid of him getting away or getting into the room and locking me out.

I stumble over something before switching on the light and see that it's someone on the floor, motionless. Two full seconds pass before I realize it's Gita with a pillowcase over her head. With the rage that fills my body I could shoot him before he knew what happened. But that's not enough.

There's no thinking as I dive on top of him, knocking him flat on his face before he can get to her. I want to put my hands around his throat. I flip him over and punch him; a satisfying crunch against my knuckles as they connect with his nose. His eyes flicker for a second before he reaches up and closes his fingers around my neck. I'm able to wiggle out of his grasp and pin one of his arms down with a knee and take his own neck in my hands. Suddenly he is every Nazi I have ever come in contact with. I squeeze. Somehow he frees his hands and starts clawing at my face, my arms.

I glance back at Gita, checking for movement. It's a mistake that costs me. He knocks me off of him and scrambles towards the gun. Lunging for his leg, I get only material that slips away from my grasp and I fall forward. In a split second he's over me with the shotgun pointing at my face.

"Now it's your turn," he hisses.

I don't think he realizes the pure hatred I have for him in that moment. He underestimates what it does to me. What his killing Gita has done to me. I duck under the gun and tackle his legs with such force that he flies backward, hitting his head on the bedpost with a sickening crack. He falls to the floor with a thud and doesn't move. The amount of blood that pools under his head shocks me and I freeze. Unsure of what to do.

I'm numb and my mind fills with a thick haze. Not the time to process.

Gita.

The sight of her on the floor, the pillowcase over her head, makes me realize I was too late. I didn't protect her like I promised. I turn her over and cradle her head, ripping off the tape, tearing off the pillowcase. Her face is white, almost gray. I yank the tape off her mouth and look for signs of breathing, but her lips are blue and her chest is still. Laying her back down, I jostle her. "Wake up, Gita. You have to. Wake up!" No movement still.

I shake her shoulders. "I'm so sorry. Wake up and I will never let anyone hurt you again. Just wake up. Lidka. Lidka." I kiss her lips and her cheek and her forehead and her neck. "Come back to me, Lidka." I rub her chest. I hug her against me. "Please. Lidka, come home."

Lidka

Chapter Forty

I hear my name. The name I wasn't sure I wanted to be called. The one that was so foreign, but that I had recalled in a fuzzy memory. Lidka. It's who I am. Who I was meant to be. The people who brought me into the world meant for me to be called that for the remainder of my days. I hear it. I go towards it. The warmth floods me and swallows me whole and I'm back with Leo.

~~~~

I stare at his body. His opened eyes.

"Don't look," Leo says.

"What are we supposed to do with him? Call the police?"

He shakes his head. "We can't. When the police look into it, they might find out I'm not who I say I am and investigate, trying to get ahold of people from back home. Which might tip off his friends who will come looking for him. We have no other choice but to get rid of any evidence."

A shiver snakes its way up my back.

"We'll bury him way out in the field. I'll go get the wheelbarrow and we'll take him out that way."

"This feels wrong. Even though I know he was going to kill us, it just all feels so wrong."

Leo takes my shoulders. "I know. But this is where we are now and we have to deal with it. I can't stand the thought of me being taken away and thrown into prison. I can't go back to another prison." Panic, or maybe it's pain, flashes in his eyes and I know he's speaking about the camp.

"I can just tell the police he broke in and tried to kill me, so I killed him."

Leo shakes his head. "They'll never believe you would have the strength to take him down in a struggle. And besides, when they contact his family or friends back in Germany, there will be too many questions. I can't risk it coming back to us. Someone else finding us." His eyes shift to Max's body before looking back at me.

"Okay. Let's hurry then."

We decide to dump his body in the small river that runs along the property, which empties into the larger Elk River. The heavy rains keep falling and swells the river to the banks' brim. We suppose his body will go undiscovered for some time. And when it is, perhaps by a fisherman, there will be no identification. No idea where he came from or at what point in the river he fell in. Perhaps the police will see the cut on the back of his head and assume he fell in, hit his head on a rock and was swept away. When all is done, we pretend he just vanished and is forgotten. Like it never happened.

~~~~

Every day for months I visualized a police car coming down my lane. Every single day I look down the lane as I pass the window.

One day, it does.

"Morning, Miss." It's the same sheriff who came to tell me my parents had been killed.

I open the door for the man. "Good morning, sir. Please come in."

Once we're seated across from each other I say, "What brings you here?" My heart thumps so violently, I worry he can see it through my dress.

"This might sound strange, but we had a call come in from Germany asking about a man name Max Roth. Is that your husband?"

"Yes." I pray my voice isn't shaking as bad as I feel it is.

"The person said Max had come to see you, but this friend hasn't heard from him since and was worried about him."

"No need to worry. I just don't want to speak to the man." Leo strolls in, flashes a light hearted smile and sits right next to me, taking my shaking hand in his.

The sheriff smiles, looking relieved. "Well, if you don't want to talk to the fellow, you might want to at least write a letter letting him know you're fine so he'll stop bothering us."

"I'll do that."

We say goodbye and wait until the car is out of sight before speaking again. "Who do you think it is?" I ask.

"Probably the friend I saw him with in your aunt's house. The good thing about this is, I don't think his friend will be getting the German police involved because then all the evidence in your aunt's murder would lead right back to him and Max. Your aunt is the connection between you and Max. I can't imagine he wants to bring any unnecessary attention to that. I'm hoping the sheriff will call and reassure him that he met with Max and everything was fine."

"Yes, but what if he or someone else decides to come looking for him?"

"We'll cross that bridge when we get there. Now, let's put this out of our minds for now. Yes?"

~~~~

We think about moving away and becoming Leo and Lidka to the outside world instead of Max and Gita. We think about getting remarried as Leo and Lidka and starting over. Perhaps one day there will be a time when returning to Poland will be a good idea too. But for now, we stay put. The farm is all I have of my parents and it's where Leo and I made a home and fell in love. So if the world sees us as Max and Gita, we can live with that as long as we remember who we are: each other's world.

Chapter Forty-One

I'm not sure what it is, but something inside me, whatever is holding on so tight to my memories, lets another one slip through. And it's beautiful.

I'm lying on my back with my dress tucked between my legs so my underwear won't show. The day is bright with big, fluffy clouds and there's laughter in the air. Josef lies next to me. He's my buddy. We are breathing hard because we just got chased out of the neighbor's garden. We only wanted to sample the peas, but the old man didn't appreciate it at all. He chased us with a hoe, shaking it wildly in the air, yelling to not let him catch us again or we'd get a spanking we wouldn't forget.

"We should go on the run," Josef says.

"Like spies. But we need a good spy name. I think I would be Harriet."

Josef laughs and says, "That's a funny one."

"What's wrong with Harriet?"

"It's an old woman's name."

I let out a huff. "Well, you think you could do better?"

"I'd be called Alfred." He smiles a big smile.

I laugh. "That's your middle name. You can't use your own name. The whole point is to be someone you're not."

His face grows serious for a moment before he says, "I would be someone different. When I get scared and need to be brave, I pretend to be Alfred. Like Papa. So if I were a spy I would have to be really brave. That's why I want to be called Alfred."

He's so intent on the name and has put so much thought into it, I can't laugh any longer.

"That's a wonderful name. I think it's just perfect." I turn back at the clouds and put my hands behind my head.

The quiet moment is broken when he reaches over and tickles my nose with a long piece of grass. I slap his hand away, then hop up and we run to the side of the house where our bikes are parked. We hop on and ride as fast as we can, my dress flying behind me. Mother would kill me if she saw me riding like this. "Wait for me!" Josef calls after me. We ride waving to friends as we pass by. We avoid going home for as long as we can, but then head back because we're thirsty.

I hear mom's voice before I see her. "Josef Alfred! Lidka! Inside now!"

We eye each other, knowing the tone in her voice and her using Josef's middle name meant she had heard from the neighbor.

We hop off our bikes and run up the stone steps. I glance back over my shoulder and see him grinning from ear to ear. He loved to get into trouble with me. It made him feel older than his six years.

It's something that brings me peace. There are times I question if the pictures in my head are real or not, but I don't let that stop me from enjoying them and playing them over and over in my head. Josef Alfred. The little boy who always said he wanted a big brother, but got me instead. Lucky for him I wanted a little brother to mother and take care of, even if he was just a year my junior. As he got older I suppose we liked getting in trouble together as well.

I'm not sure why I don't have more memories of my parents. Maybe my subconscious realizes if I don't remember them I can't fully grieve their loss. So it lessens the pain a little.

I open my eyes and it's a day like the one in my memory. The porch swing sways as I get up and saunter over to Leo. He's been sketching, sitting on the porch step. When he sees me, he lifts his pad and invites me onto his lap. I accept the invitation and he wraps his arms around me.

"Let's see what you've been working on." I go to grab the pad but he pulls it out of my reach.

"What do I get if I show it to you?" He waggles his eyebrows and I plant one on him. When I pull back, he hands me the pad and says, "Okay. I'll take that."

I laugh a little and then flip open the sketch pad. My breath catches in my throat as I study the face harder.

"What's wrong?" Leo asks, worry creasing his eyes.

"Who is this?" It can't be.

"He's a boy I knew at the camp. I've been thinking about him a lot lately."

My hands begin to shake. "Was his name Josef?"

"No. It was a boy named Alfred."

A lump settles in my throat. My eyes devour the sketch. There's so much sadness in the boy's eyes. "It's my Josef." I run a finger over the charcoaled forehead, down the eyes.

Leo begins to shake his head, but then stops. "What do you mean?"

"It's my brother. Josef Alfred. He called himself Alfred when he was scared."

"Do you really think it's him?"

My heart pounds in response. "It's him. Did you know him well? What happened to him?" Sudden hope blooms in my chest that he escaped with Leo. That he was on that truck my father drove out of the camp.

"I did know him. He was in the bunk next to me. We were friends. He was my only friend there." Emotion chokes his words, not letting them come freely. His eyes tear up and I know. Leo shakes his head and my hope turns to a giant stone crushing my chest.

I close my eyes, lay my head against Leo and see Josef running after me in the field. His smile is as wide as the crescent moon and as bright as the sun. I feel the sun on my face and remember it's the same sun that warmed us those many years ago as we hid from the neighbor. I feel Leo's hand in mine and imagine it's the same hand that held Josef's, my buddy. The memory is a gift. A gift I will open every time I miss him.

I sigh and Leo's grip tightens on me.

"Remember that night after the fair? Where did you say heaven was again? It was so beautiful."

"Of course I remember that night. I said I believe heaven is on the other side of the stars."

I nod. "Thank you."

His lips press against my hair. "For what?"

"For giving me a little piece from the other side of the stars today."

And I thank the other side of the stars for giving me Leo.

THE END

Acknowledgements

First and foremost I want to thank my Heavenly Father and my Savior, Jesus Christ. Everything I have been blessed with in this life is because of Them.

They say it takes a village to raise a child and this book is definitely a baby of mine. So here's to all my villagers:

To my family, thank you. Thank you for supporting me in my dreams and never doubting me. Lily, Riley, and Addy, you all make me want to keep going in hopes that you realize it's possible to dream big. You give me a piece of "the other side of the stars" every day. I love you.

To my parents, Deborah and Montie, and in-laws, Pat and Bill. Thank you for your never-ending encouragement and support and for all the babysitting and picking up of kids from school. I couldn't have done this without your support as well.

A special thanks to my mother, Deborah, for giving me your love of reading and writing.

And to some of my favorite villagers of all. The Writing Group of Joy and Awesomeness. Ruth Josse, Chantele

Sedgwick, Kim Krey, Jeigh Meredith, Christene Houston, Donna Nolan, Peggy Eddleman, Julie Donaldson, Erin Summerill, Jessie Humphries, Sandy Ponton. You all rock my world with what amazing women you are. You're inspiring, talented, salt-of-the-earth ladies. You're my "people" and every time we get together I realize how blessed I am to have you all in my life.

Thank you a million times to my beta readers and friends. Chantele Sedgwick, Ruth Josse, Kim Krey, Christene Houston, Jeigh Meredith, Suzanne Ray, and Kim Hollis. Thanks for the time and effort you put into reading and giving me feedback. I love you all!

Ruth and Chantele, my critique group. I feel so blessed to have you as friends, partners in this crazy journey, and on many occasions, my therapists. Your encouragement and advice is more than I could have ever asked for. From the bottom of my heart, thank you!

Thank you to Katie Johnson, my editor, who loved this book and cleaned it up. You were the first person outside my circle to tell me you loved my book, which in case you didn't know, is huge.

Also, to my very first reader when I was still a closet writer. My sister, Rachel. Thank you for not telling me to ditch the dream when you read my mess of a book. I owe you a lot for that!

And to anyone reading this book, thank you!

Finally, regarding the Holocaust; it was not an easy topic to tackle. First, because how deeply horrifying it was and also because as a writer I want to be respectful of those who lost their lives, those who survived, and all those who were directly affected by it. But I feel it's important that we never forget. That we let ourselves go there and feel the pain. Because we get that, right? Pain. We all understand it. I think that's what makes us good human beings; to feel so deeply. Perhaps if we allow ourselves to remember the pain of the people in the past, we can be kinder, better to the people in our present.

About the Author

Katherine was born and raised in Utah where she still resides with her amazing family. She finds joy in everyday life, good food, good people and beautiful words. The Other Side of the Stars is her debut book. To connect, find her on Facebook or Twitter @KatherineKing_1.

23881800R00158

Made in the USA
San Bernardino, CA
03 September 2015